LOVERS OF FRANZ K.

Also by Burhan Sönmez in English translation

Stone and Shadow
Labyrinth
Istanbul Istanbul
Sins and Innocents

BURHAN SÖNMEZ

Lovers of Franz K.

Translated from the Kurdish by
Sami Hêzil

OPEN BORDERS PRESS
LONDON

Originally published in Kurdish as *Evîndarên Franz K.*
in 2024 by Lîs Yayınevi, Diyarbakır, Turkey

First published in Great Britain in 2025 by
Open Borders Press
an imprint of
Orenda Books
London
www.openborderspress.co.uk

9 8 7 6 5 4 3 2 1

The lines from Louis Aragon's *Elsa* (Gallimard, 1959) in the last chapter
are translated from the French by Antonia Phinnemore

A CIP catalogue record for this book is available from the British Library

ISBN (HB) 978-1-916788-72-5

Designed and typeset in Adobe Garamond by Libanus Press Ltd
Printed and bound in Great Britain by
CPI Group (UK) Ltd, Croydon, CR0 4YY

"You loved him when he was alive and you loved him after. If you love him, it is not a sin to kill him. Or is it more?"

ERNEST HEMINGWAY, *The Old Man and the Sea*

"What! Would you burn my books?"

CERVANTES, *Don Quixote*

1

WEST BERLIN
POLICE STATION

Berlin is a city divided by a wall down the middle. People living there in the summer of 1968 are staring at the long wall and are complaining about the weather getting warmer and buses running late.

The interrogation room in the basement of the police station in Friesenstrasse is cool. Stone walls spread damp in the room.

Kommissar Müller sits across from the suspect Ferdy Kaplan, lighting a cigarette and blowing out the smoke. He mutters to himself as he examines the papers spread on the desk.

Kommissar Müller: "Yes, the name used in the passport . . ."

Ferdy Kaplan: "Used? That is my real name, Ferdy Kaplan. But it does not matter."

Kommissar Müller: "What does not matter?"

Ferdy Kaplan: "My name . . ."

Kommissar Müller: "Why not?"

Ferdy Kaplan: "The explanation is on the papers in front of you. There you can find the answers to your questions."

Kommissar Müller: "If only it were so, Herr Kaplan. We will get answers to some questions from you, won't we, boys?"

[*The other three police officers in the room laugh.*]

Ferdy Kaplan: "You want to know where I got the gun and from whom, don't you?"

Kommissar Müller: "We will get there. According to this file, you are staying in the Steglitz neighbourhood. Your mother is German, your father is Turkish. You appear to live in Istanbul, and you frequently visit Paris. Tell me first when you arrived in Berlin."

Ferdy Kaplan: "I was born here. I am from here. Do not speak to me as if I were a foreigner."

Kommissar Müller: "You are from here, but mostly you live elsewhere."

Ferdy Kaplan: "That is not a crime. If you had lived in other places, perhaps you would have found yourselves better professions."

[*Ferdy Kaplan looks towards the police officer taking notes at the next table.*]

Kommissar Müller: "We have no complaints about our profession. We are in a better situation than you are. Think of yourself, not us."

Ferdy Kaplan: "I am happy with the chair I am in."

Kommissar Müller: "How can you be so sure of yourself?"

Ferdy Kaplan: "I can tell you if you would like to hear."

Kommissar Müller: "Oh, can you?"

8

Ferdy Kaplan: "Yes, let me explain."

Kommissar Müller: "Well then . . ."

Ferdy Kaplan: "Where would you like me to start?"

Kommissar Müller: "Why don't you start with your origin? *Kaplan* is a Jewish name . . .

Ferdy Kaplan: "No, it is a popular surname in Turkey. It means *tiger* in Turkish."

Kommissar Müller: "Tell me about your mother and father . . . People like you are rare."

Ferdy Kaplan: "What do you mean?"

Kommissar Müller: "Suspects are mostly tight-lipped; they are not inclined to speak openly."

Ferdy Kaplan: "People without belief behave that way. They are afraid of talking."

Kommissar Müller: "Is there a belief in committing a crime?"

Ferdy Kaplan: "I don't think I did commit a crime. I only did what I believed in. I did what had to be done."

Kommissar Müller: "You did what had to be done, is that so? I am curious to know how you plan to explain all this."

Ferdy Kaplan: "Everything I will say is already in your records, you don't need to take notes. [*Ferdy Kaplan glances at the police officer taking notes on the next table.*] My mother was a Nazi supporter. My Turkish father shared her views. They died here in a Soviet bombardment in the last days of the war. My grandfather rescued me from the ruins. When my grandfather fell ill with his kidneys, he must have realised that he had not long to live, and he sent me off one year later to my father's family in Istanbul."

For a boy of ten, who had come from a Berlin reduced to rubble, Istanbul was a magical place. Ferdy looked up at the ever-changing colours of the sky between the towers, domes and city walls. He immersed himself in the bustling bazaars and watched the joy in people's faces. He listened to the sound of horse-drawn carriages, suburban trains and ferry boats. The sea, which he could not have dreamt of during the war, was on one side, and his grandparents were on the other. There was no fear of death. His grandfather and grandmother embraced their grandson as if he were a gift from God. They made him a bed on the floor of their room. At night they would tell him the fairy tales they had once told their own son and listen to Ferdy's familiar breathing.

As Ferdy got better at speaking Turkish, he got used to the ridicule of some of the kids at school and the excessive attention of others. His German identity brought together two opposing sides of his life. His closest friend was Amalya. Unlike other girls, she would confront boys and protect Ferdy. Sometimes she would walk all the way home with him. One day, when Ferdy's headaches returned, they sat down among the trees. Amalya touched Ferdy's right temple, then kissed him on the cheek. It took a week for Ferdy to show the same courage and return the kiss. They often played away from the other children. They would hide among the rocks on the Kumkapı shore or by the old city walls in the Yedikule vegetable gardens. They would sing songs and read books together. Ferdy began to draw pictures again. He would draw the fishing boats, the flocks of seagulls, the setting sun. Amalya would ask why his drawings did not look like normal pictures. The boats would be awry, the wings of seagulls broken, and the sunlight blurred. Ferdy drew Amalya's smiling face, her serene face, her sleepy face.

When Amalya was fifteen she moved to France with her mother. (As Ferdy Kaplan recounts his story, he makes no mention of Amalya.) Ferdy's grandfather died in the same year. His heart stopped suddenly while he was in conversation with a customer at his fish stall in Kumkapı. They buried him in the cemetery by the old city walls at Topkapı. In the first year, Ferdy and his grandmother visited his grave every Friday. As time passed, they would visit him twice a year, on religious festivals. Life sped by. Ferdy tried to keep pace with it and grow up as quickly as possible. He would go to school in the mornings and help his grandmother on the fish stall in the afternoons. He began to learn about politics, listening in on the conversations of fishermen. The party founded by the conservatives had come to power. Politically the country was in disarray, with bridges being broken between the government and the opposition party. Nobody realised they were on the path to a military coup. Amalya, who had left the country when the new government was formed, returned ten years later to find the government shaken to its foundations. This was right at the peak of the protests. Despite the passing of so many years, Ferdy recognised Amalya in the crowd when he saw her at one of the demonstrations.

Kommissar Müller: "How did the political turmoil affect your life? Perhaps it is the reason you are now in a police station . . ."

Ferdy Kaplan: "Everything had an effect on me: the war that ruined Germany, the political unrest that shook Turkey, the events that rocked France . . ."

Kommissar Müller: "France, yes. Were you in Paris during the protests in May?"

Ferdy Kaplan: "Everybody was there."

Kommissar Müller: "So, when did you come here?"

Ferdy Kaplan: "I came a week ago."

Kommissar Müller: "That is interesting. How could you leave Paris and come to Berlin when it was seething with the mad fever of youth? Why?"

Ferdy Kaplan: "But isn't it, as you put it, seething here too?"

Kommissar Müller: "Did you return for that reason?"

Ferdy Kaplan: "You don't need a reason to come home . . ."

Kommissar Müller: "If you killed someone, well, you will need a reason."

Ferdy Kaplan: "I come to Berlin every year."

Kommissar Müller: "So, did you come here directly, or did you stop off first in East Berlin?"

Ferdy Kaplan: "I did not go to the East at all."

Kommissar Müller: "You mean you have never been there in your whole life?"

Ferdy Kaplan: "Since Berlin has been divided, I have not been to the East."

Kommissar Müller: "Why? Having grown up in this city, have you never wondered how things are on the other side?"

Ferdy Kaplan: "When I come to Berlin I stay on this side of the border. Our house is here. My maternal grandfather's grave is here."

Kommissar Müller: "Your neighbourhood is close to the border, but you haven't thought about crossing to the other side. Do you expect us to believe that?"

Ferdy Kaplan: "I expect nothing from you."

Kommissar Müller: "You killed a student, Herr Kaplan. We will see in what way it is related to the border and the other side of the Wall."

Ferdy Kaplan: "It has nothing to do with the border and the Wall."

Kommissar Müller: "It is our job to assume the opposite of what you are telling us."

Ferdy Kaplan: "I am telling you the truth. Everything I say is as true as my identity and the crime I committed."

Kommissar Müller: "Then why did you kill the student?"

Ferdy Kaplan: "Why do you keep calling him the student? Doesn't he have a name?"

Kommissar Müller: "Don't you know who he is? Are you a hired killer, murdering people not known to you?"

Ferdy Kaplan: "I do not kill for money."

Kommissar Müller: "What would you kill for?"

Ferdy Kaplan: "May I have a cigarette?"

Kommissar Müller: "Later. For now, let's see how the matter developed. [*Kommissar Müller turns to the bearded police officer who is standing by the wall.*] You tell us how it happened."

Bearded Police Officer: "Yesterday evening, I was in front of the Central Library. I heard screams from the bus station across the street. I ran over. I saw this man, and a woman with him. Both were holding guns. They shot a university student waiting at the bus stop. The student fell lifeless to the ground. An elderly man at the bus stop was also injured in the shooting. When I shouted, the attackers started running. I followed and caught up with them. When Ferdy Kaplan realised they could not escape me, he stood behind a tree and shot at me. He wanted to give the woman with him a chance to disappear. I took cover behind a building and I shot at him. When he had no bullets left, I went over and arrested him. By this time the woman had got away."

Kommissar Müller: "Is this how it happened?"

Ferdy Kaplan: "How can it be possible that your officer sees so clearly in the dark? It has no credibility. I was alone there. I don't know the woman who was running beside me. She must be someone who panicked and started running."

Bearded Police Officer: "We collected the bullet casings: the total number exceeds what your gun's magazine can hold. That means not one gun was used but two. The other gun was carried by that woman, wasn't it?"

Ferdy Kaplan: "I had two guns. When the magazine of the first gun was empty, I threw it into the bushes and used the second one."

Bearded Police Officer: "We searched every corner, but found no other weapon. We are sure that woman was with you."

Ferdy Kaplan: "If you are so sure, then speak to her."

Bearded Police Officer: "We will speak to her when we catch her."

Ferdy Kaplan: "That means you couldn't catch her . . ."

[*The room falls silent. They all look at one another.*]

Kommissar Müller: "We will find her soon enough and we will question her too, in this room."

Ferdy Kaplan: "You are wasting your time."

Kommissar Müller: "Don't concern yourself with our time."

Ferdy Kaplan: "If you are using your time wisely, then how have you not yet identified who that young student was?"

Kommissar Müller: "What makes you think we don't know who he was? We know, as you do, that his name was Ernest Fischer. With regard to his studies, he was a good student. We gather he took part in a couple of demonstrations, but he does not seem to us so prominent a person as to be a target of such an attack. Is there anything you can tell us about him that we do not yet know?"

Ferdy Kaplan: "I would tell you if I knew."

Kommissar Müller: "Were you involved in the other attacks against the students? For example, the attack that took place in April?"

Ferdy Kaplan: "Do you mean the attack in which Rudi Dutschke was injured? The suspect in that attack was caught, was he not?"

Kommissar Müller: "Then you must also have known the student who was killed last year."

Ferdy Kaplan: "Benno Ohnesorg, yes."

Kommissar Müller: "I see you take a close interest in these incidents."

Ferdy Kaplan: "There is nothing unusual in that. Every detail appeared in the press, even in the Paris newspapers, and Istanbul reported the incident."

Kommissar Müller: "That is correct. It made a little too much noise."

Ferdy Kaplan: "But weren't the police the perpetrators of the murder last year?"

Kommissar Müller: "It may seem that way, but we suspect there is a network behind that incident that we are not yet aware of."

Ferdy Kaplan: "It's good that you suspect an unknown network among your own officers. But it was your attack on the student demonstrations that led to all this. Because the students were protesting against the Shah of Iran, you turned it into a battlefield. In order for the dictator of Iran to listen to Mozart's 'Magic Flute' in the Alte Oper, you were at his full service . . ."

Kommissar Müller: "Our duty is to maintain public order, so that people can go about their daily lives."

Ferdy Kaplan: "Is that why you killed a student?"

Kommissar Müller: "Why did *you* kill a student, Herr Kaplan?"

Ferdy Kaplan: "Those are completely different things."

Kommissar Müller: "Oh, of course, you killed him on purpose, you did it in a prepared and well thought-out manner. In that case, they are entirely different things."

Ferdy Kaplan: "If you knew the content of the matter, you wouldn't speak of it in such terms."

Kommissar Müller: "Indeed. The content of the matter. Explain that to us."

Ferdy Kaplan: "All the explanations you need are written on the papers in front of you."

Kommissar Müller: "No, there is no information here other than the normal life of a student. Tell us what was special about this young man that we haven't yet worked out?"

Ferdy Kaplan: "I only know what is already known to you. I don't know anything else."

Kommissar Müller: "Well, you keep up your little game. We have looked into Ernest Fischer's political connections. We have established that he was not a member of the Student Union of German Socialists. We don't know whether he joined an illegal group, a newly formed one that we haven't yet identified. We are investigating any possible connections he may have had with the other murdered students. As soon as we get the first piece of evidence, we will discover your links to those attacks. I believe your crimes go that far."

Ferdy Kaplan: "Carry out your research. You will see that I had nothing to do with the two other events. I was not in the country on those days. You can check the records of my entering and leaving."

Kommissar Müller: "Ernest Fischer's father and mother both work in the iron factory. Ernest was a good student, much loved by his friends. I wonder if some form of jealousy is the cause of all this? Could your woman friend who fled the scene have something to do with the murder?"

Ferdy Kaplan: "Nonsense."

Kommissar Müller: "You must have a reason that is not nonsense. Why did you kill him?"

Ferdy Kaplan: "May I have a cigarette?"

Kommissar Müller: "It is obvious you will not confess. When we began, I thought you might speak openly."

Ferdy Kaplan: "I have told you what I know. How can I tell you things I don't know?"

Kommissar Müller: "We will soon find out. We are investigating whether Ernest Fischer, or his family, has any connection with Turkey."

Ferdy Kaplan: "That is a waste of time."

Kommissar Müller: "Tell us, then, how not to waste our time."

Ferdy Kaplan: "Alright, let me tell you. Move away from the points you are focusing on, forget the questions you asked me. If you avoid such mistakes, you will save time."

Kommissar Müller: "I have no faith in these words of yours. You must try a little harder to convince us."

Ferdy Kaplan: "Alright, carry on researching old murders, follow the connections to East Berlin and Istanbul. You know best. But you won't find a single crumb."

Kommissar Müller: "I would very much like to believe you . . ."

Ferdy Kaplan: "In time you will realise I am telling you the truth."

Kommissar Müller: "Do not doubt our ability, Herr Kaplan."

Ferdy Kaplan: "Was the student's name Fischer? Please pass on my condolences to his mother and father. Will you do that for me?"

Kommissar Müller: "You are offering your condolences? To the family of the person you killed?"

Ferdy Kaplan: "Yes."

Kommissar Müller: "You cannot be in your right mind."

Ferdy Kaplan: "I am quite clear in my mind; that is why I offer my condolences to the Fischer family. But in view of what has happened, they will not mean much."

Kommissar Müller: "How strange . . ."

2

WEST BERLIN
COURTROOM

Fearing there may be unrest as the result of an armed attack on a student, the police announce to the press that this was a crime of passion. In fact, the police are searching for concrete leads, including a link with East Germany or the youth protests in France.

One week later, Ferdy Kaplan is taken from Tegel Prison to the courthouse in Moabit. He is brought before a panel of three judges. The senior judge confirms his identity, then gives the floor to the prosecutor.

Prosecutor: "Herr Richter! The defendant, Ferdy Kaplan, was arrested for the murder of a twenty-year-old student. The brave officers of our police force caught him red-handed, but we still don't know the reason for the attack. Whether we discover the reason or not, the death of one Ernest Fischer is a fact. The defendant Ferdy Kaplan . . ."

Judge: "Has the defendant admitted the murder charge?"

Prosecutor: "Yes."

Ferdy Kaplan: "Yes."

Judge: "Herr Kaplan, I didn't ask you. You are the defendant. You will not speak without my permission."

Ferdy Kaplan: "I wasn't responding to you, I only . . . [*Ferdy Kaplan turns towards the public gallery and looks at a couple sitting hand in hand, weariness on their faces.*] With your permission, I would like to offer my condolences to the family of the young man who died. You must be the Fischer family . . . [*The middle-aged man and woman lift their gaze and give him a sorrowful look.*] Frau Fischer! Herr Fischer! I am very sorry about the death of your son. Please accept my sincere apologies." [*Tears fill Frau Fischer's eyes. Her husband puts his arm around her shoulder.*]

Prosecutor: "This is ridiculous . . . Herr Richter![1] The defendant wants to turn this room into a theatre stage."

Ferdy Kaplan: "I would act much better if that was my intention. I was expressing my genuine sadness. I have no expectation that the court will approve my feelings. If Herr and Frau Fischer believe me even a little, then that will be enough for me. I am a man of truth, not a man of tricks."

Prosecutor: "A man of truth, you?"

Ferdy Kaplan: "Yes, me . . ."

Judge: "That's enough. Herr Kaplan! I warn you. I don't want any theatricals in my court. The case will proceed by the rules."

Ferdy Kaplan: "Herr Richter, I am not trying to cause trouble. But I would like it recorded that I bow my head in respect for the young soul of Ernest Fischer."

---

1 Herr Richter is the German term, equivalent to "Your Honour", used in the 1960s when addressing a judge.

[Ferdy Kaplan looks at the court clerk sitting across from him. The court clerk stops writing for a moment, waiting for confirmation from the judge.]

Judge: "Have no fear. Whatever you say will be recorded." *[The clatter of the typewriter starts up again.]*

Ferdy Kaplan: "Also . . ."

Judge: "Yes?"

Ferdy Kaplan: "I have been incarcerated for a week. When I asked for a cigarette my request was ignored."

Judge: "During a break in the hearing you may smoke a cigarette. *[The judge turns to the usher and gives him the instruction.]* Now, Herr Kaplan, you are hereby being tried for murder, this is a serious case. Be quiet and await your turn."

Ferdy Kaplan: "Of course. I can assure you that it will be a proper hearing."

Judge: "Herr Staatsanwalt,[2] please continue, you were speaking about the student . . ."

Prosecutor: "Ernest Fischer, he was a student at the Free University of Berlin, studying at the Institute of Biology."

Judge: "On the day of the event there was no student protest, am I right?"

Prosecutor: "That is correct, Herr Richter. Although it was the holidays, almost every day there were protests, but on the day of the incident it was quiet. Ernest Fischer went to the library in the morning and remained there until the evening. When he left, he went to the bus stop opposite the library and waited for his bus."

---

2 Herr Staatsanwalt is the German term used to address a prosecutor.

Judge: "Was he alone? Any friends . . ."

Prosecutor: "He was alone, but there were two assailants. As well as the defendant Ferdy Kaplan, there was a woman. We have not yet been able to ascertain her identity. She took advantage of the darkness and escaped. She was in her thirties, had short hair . . ."

Ferdy Kaplan: "Herr Staatsanwalt . . ."

Prosecutor: "Yes?"

Ferdy Kaplan: "I wish you would focus on what matters rather than pay attention to the hair of someone who has no connection with me. You are being neglectful by looking towards the assailant instead of towards the victim."

Prosecutor: "We are not here to play with words. Either you confess your accomplice, or you will feel the full weight of the law."

Ferdy Kaplan: "Justice . . ."

Prosecutor: "Are you belittling it? Killing a student and injuring an old man are not crimes that we belittle at the court of justice."

Ferdy Kaplan: "No, I would never make light of justice. I believe in it at all times."

Prosecutor: "We are giving you the opportunity to be speak openly here. Tell us, in the presence of the court and the victim's family, why you committed this murder, who were your collaborators, and who was the woman with you during the assault."

Ferdy Kaplan: "You keep circling around the same narrow spot. Anything I say will not count, in your view."

Prosecutor: "Try if you will, try to tell us something we do not know."

Ferdy Kaplan: "Well, then, I will tell you, if you are so keen to hear."

Prosecutor: "Please, if you could . . ."

Ferdy Kaplan: "Someone was wounded at the scene, right?"

Prosecutor: "An elderly man."

Ferdy Kaplan: "Yes, him."

Prosecutor: "Well, what has that to do with it?"

Ferdy Kaplan: "Do you have a description of him in your notes?"

Prosecutor: "A description?"

Ferdy Kaplan: "Yes, such as his having a humped back?"

Prosecutor: "Humped back?" [*The prosecutor glances at the papers in front of him.*] "What is the significance of that?"

Ferdy Kaplan: "But you are assuming that the short hair of a woman who panicked and ran away in the dark is significant, is that not so?"

For research relating to her PhD. in urban architecture at the Sorbonne, Amalya returned to Istanbul, the city of her childhood. As soon as she arrived, instead of visiting the shores of the Bosphorus, she went to her old neighbourhood. She saw that Kumkapı was demolished and torn apart from right to left. The fisherman's market on the waterfront had been erased and an asphalt road laid out in its place. The vegetable gardens under the city walls had been filled with newly constructed buildings. The colour of the city had changed, the shade of the trees had vanished. "What have they done to my neighbourhood?" Amalya came across some old acquaintances among the concrete buildings that had replaced the ornate wooden houses. She discovered that Ferdy's grandmother had died and

23

that Ferdy had left the neighbourhood. What makes cities change faster, the demolishment of buildings, or departure of friends? Amalya wandered around for a few days, seeking the familiar smells of her childhood. She boarded the suburban train and travelled back and forth along the thousand-year-old city walls of Istanbul. Visiting Sirkeci, Samatya and Bakırköy, she thought that the new developments not only erased memories of the city, but also annihilated its beauty. She sent a letter to her mother. "Eliz," she wrote, addressing her by her first name as always, "if you want to die happy, never see the new face of Istanbul; rely on your memories."

On the day she posted the letter she ran into a protest march. Young and old, men and women, all were advancing towards a square, and on the way their number was swelled by newcomers. Amalya joined the crowd and chanted anti-government slogans, polishing her rusty Turkish by shouting along with the people. The Istanbul she had left behind and the one she had returned to were two entirely different places. When the crowd flowed into Beyazıt Square, it resembled a big forest. Amalya became one with people she did not know. She swayed like all the others. When someone approached her from behind and grabbed her by the wrist, she was startled. At first, she thought he was a plain-clothes policeman, but then she recognised him. "Ferdy . . ." They didn't get a chance to speak in the sudden turmoil of the crowd. As a result of the police response to the demonstration, one person died and many were detained. When they met the next morning, Amalya hugged Ferdy tightly and kissed him on the cheek, recalling in this way the old days.

It was then she noticed the hesitancy in Ferdy's reaction and the engagement ring on his finger.

Those were beautiful spring days. They wandered around, visiting places they knew. Old locations. Old names. Stories and laughter. Who knew when they would meet again? Two days later, when she was leaving for Paris, Amalya looked forward to seeing Ferdy at the airport, but Ferdy did not turn up to see her off and say goodbye, even though he had promised.

Prosecutor: "You avoid mentioning the name of the woman with you. You pretend that such a person does not exist. But we have witnesses to the incident and the bullet casings collected at the scene . . ."

Ferdy Kaplan: "And you are going after a woman who fled in the dark, while you do not know the person standing in front of you."

Prosecutor: "Who is it that we do not know? You?"

Ferdy Kaplan: "Oh God, look at these men who are trying me here . . . Is this what I deserve?"

Prosecutor: "Herr Kaplan, your words . . ."

Frau Fischer: "Why my son? Why?"

[*When they hear her voice, they all turn around and look at Frau Fischer. The courtroom is silent for a moment.*]

Ferdy Kaplan: "For days I have been wondering the same thing, Frau Fischer. I keep asking myself the same question: Why?"

Frau Fischer: "Every night I wait for my son, I keep expecting him to appear. But he doesn't. Damn you!"

Ferdy Kaplan: "I am sincerely apologising to you, again."

Frau Fischer: "Why my son?"

Ferdy Kaplan: "I am going to write a letter to him."

Frau Fischer: "What letter are you talking about? You murderer!"

[*Frau Fischer begins to sob loudly.*]

Prosecutor: "Frau Fischer, our court will deliver justice. This man will receive the punishment he deserves."

Frau Fischer: "I don't care about justice. I want my son."

Prosecutor: "I understand your loss, your grief. But only justice can lead us to the truth. Your son's soul, too, is looking forward to that truth."

Frau Fischer: "Herr Staatsanwalt, when you mention the truth, I don't know what you mean. Will it bring my son back to me?"

Prosecutor: "I do understand your feelings, Frau Fischer . . ."

Ferdy Kaplan: "With your permission, may I ask Frau Fischer a question?"

[*The prosecutor first looks at Ferdy Kaplan, then turns to the judge.*]

Prosecutor: "Herr Richter?"

Judge: "Yes, he may ask."

Ferdy Kaplan: "Thank you, Herr Richter."

Judge: "Be brief."

Ferdy Kaplan: "Frau Fischer, why did you give the name Ernest to your son? In Germany this name is spelled Ernst; it does not include the letter *e*."

Prosecutor: "Herr Kaplan . . ."

Ferdy Kaplan: "Yes . . . ?"

Prosecutor: "What kind of a question is that? Your behaviour is becoming more and more abnormal."

Ferdy Kaplan: "I suppose it is an official duty of prosecutors to find defendants abnormal."

Prosecutor: "The question has no significance. Frau Fischer is not obliged to answer it."

Ferdy Kaplan: "Every single letter of our names has a significance. If only you knew how much I suffered for the sake of just one letter."

Herr Fischer: "Herr Staatsanwalt, if you permit me, I can explain."

Prosecutor: "Alright, Herr Fischer, please go ahead."

Herr Fischer: "When my wife and I were newly married, we hid an American soldier in our home. It was the last year of the war. He had escaped from prison. As he was trying to escape, he was shot and injured. We did our best, but he lived only a couple of weeks. His name was Ernest, or that was what he told us. When our son was born, we gave him that name."

Ferdy Kaplan: "Thank you, Herr Fischer. I hope your son did not suffer much due to that extra letter in his name."

Herr Fischer: "What kind of suffering? I do not understand."

Prosecutor: "Herr Kaplan, what is your intention? I am beginning to doubt your sanity. We came across such things in the other attacks against students. I may ask to refer you for a psychiatric examination."

Ferdy Kaplan: "You are confusing me with Bachmann?"

Prosecutor: "You are talking about Bachmann who wounded the student leader Rudi Dutschke, are you not? So, you know him . . ."

Ferdy Kaplan: "No, I do not know him, I have heard his name. I do not want to be treated in the same way as such a person."

Prosecutor: "How do you know what kind of person he is?"

Ferdy Kaplan: "Is there anyone who does not know him?"

Prosecutor: "Are you members of the same organisation?"

Ferdy Kaplan: "Herr Staatsanwalt, your police officers have asked me this question several times."

Prosecutor: "But you did not give them any information."

Ferdy Kaplan: "What would I give them?"

Prosecutor: "Your methods and target resemble those of Bachmann. Although he is not as successful as you . . ."

Ferdy Kaplan: "Those are entirely different incidents. He is an anti-communist psychopath."

Prosecutor: "What about you then, what are you?"

Ferdy Kaplan: "I am neither an anti-communist nor a psychopath."

Prosecutor: "Those who commit a murder always refuse such appellations."

Ferdy Kaplan: "I told your police officers, and I will tell you too, that I consider every question on this subject to be an insult."

Prosecutor: "Since you are trying to evade the question, we may assume that you do indeed have a connection with Bachmann."

Ferdy Kaplan: "I am not evading anything."

Prosecutor: "Well, this is a sensitive area. We will go deeper into this. In a few days, when we obtain some concrete data, you will not be able to deny it so easily."

Ferdy Kaplan: "Search as much as you like, you will still be on the wrong track."

Prosecutor: "And what is the right track? Tell us, then: how can we uncover the truth?"

Ferdy Kaplan: "As I said, you have no concrete evidence. All you need do is change your point of view."

Prosecutor: "Herr Kaplan, please be more specific."

Ferdy Kaplan: "Alright. First, remove your focus from me. Remove it also from the student who died. Try looking somewhere else."

Prosecutor: "Where else, for example? Shall we focus on your partner who escaped in the dark?"

Ferdy Kaplan: "The same tale, once again. Since you are concerning yourself with an unknown woman, you have no idea about the humped back of the old man who was wounded."

Prosecutor: "You have already said this."

Ferdy Kaplan: "Let me tell you something new then, or, rather, let me ask you."

Prosecutor: "What will you ask about?"

Ferdy Kaplan: "Herr Staatsanwalt, you have no knowledge of what kind of man he was and you cannot describe him. Do you even know his name?"

Prosecutor: "The wounded man?"

Ferdy Kaplan: "Yes."

Prosecutor: "His name . . . [*The prosecutor riffles through the papers before him, looking nervous.*] His name . . . I think he was a tourist . . ."

Ferdy Kaplan: "Brod."

Prosecutor: "Excuse me?"

Ferdy Kaplan: "The old man."

Prosecutor: "Do you know him?"

Ferdy Kaplan: "It would seem you don't know who he is."

Prosecutor: "Here it is, I have found it: Max Brod . . ."

Ferdy Kaplan: "Fools."

3

WEST BERLIN
COURTROOM

When it transpires that the wounded man is a notable author, the prosecutor and police spend the night assessing this new development. They are making "urgent" coded phone calls to Tel Aviv, Istanbul and Prague. Max Brod was born in Prague. When the Nazis occupied Prague about 30 years ago, he moved to Tel Aviv and settled there. He is now in Germany for a short visit to talk about his friend Franz Kafka. On his deathbed, Kafka left his notebooks and papers to Brod, with instructions in his Will that all of them be burned. Max Brod decided, instead, to publish all his works.

The police are not releasing Max Brod's name to the press. It is clear that West Germany, while trying to alleviate the suffering of the war, will be put in a difficult situation by the news of the shooting of an Israeli Jewish author whose books had previously been burned here. For this reason, there are no journalists at the hearing the next day.

Judge: "Herr Kaplan, do you still stand by your decision not to engage a lawyer?"

Ferdy Kaplan: "I do not need any legal assistance. But thank you for asking."

Judge: "How does the prosecution view this decision?"

Prosecutor: "The defendant's decision stems from his arrogance. In view of the new information we have obtained, we believe he needs legal assistance more than ever. However, it is his right under the law to do without legal representation."

Judge: "You have not submitted the new findings you mention."

Prosecutor: "We were not able to complete them until just before the hearing began. Here they are, Herr Richter."

Judge: "Well . . . That's alright . . . I see new allegations here. You may proceed."

Prosecutor: "The files contain the information that the parents of the defendant were Nazi supporters who died in Berlin during the war. It is understood that the defendant was brought up by his parents until the age of nine, that he was influenced by their ideas and anti-Semitic sentiments. We know now that the target of the attack last week was, in fact, Max Brod. It appears that the student Ernest Fischer was killed by accident."

Judge: "Are you sure of that? Is it not possible that both of those men were targets? Perhaps there is a connection between Ernest Fischer and Max Brod . . ."

Prosecutor: "Alongside our investigations here, we contacted the police in Tel Aviv and Prague. We have received no information of a possible connection between Ernest Fischer and Herr Brod."

Judge: "You mean to say that a young student lost his life through misfortune . . . Are you sure of that?"

Prosecutor: "Yes."

[*Frau Fischer's cries are heard in the courtroom. Herr Fischer takes her by the arm, and they leave the room together.*]

Judge: "What was the background of Ernest Fischer? Was he also a Jew?"

Prosecutor: "We checked the identity and immigration records and found no trace of Jews in the Fischer family. They are a purely German family."

Judge: "Purely . . . What do you mean by that?"

Prosecutor: "I mean, they are a normal German family with a Catholic background. They were originally from Frankfurt, and they migrated to Berlin three generations ago . . ."

Judge: "Does this mean that the attack on Max Brod was carried out with racist motives?"

Prosecutor: "That is what we think. It seems that an anti-Semitic group has begun a campaign of aggression against prominent writers and intellectuals, and they selected Max Brod as their first target. It would be a good start for them. Herr Brod is someone who fled the Nazis during the war and settled in the country now known as Israel. He is recognised not only for his writing, but also for his dedication to the Zionist ideal."

Judge: "Of these two characteristics, his writing and his Zionism, I understand it was the latter that made him a target. Am I right?"

Prosecutor: "That is how we see it, Herr Richter. Herr Brod is committed to his faith and his nation. He believes that Palestine is the historic land promised to the Jews. This makes him a prime target for the Aryan supremacist groups."

33

Judge: "Why was Berlin chosen as the location for the attack?"

Prosecutor: "We think that the attack was carried out here to revive memories of Germany's past. They were perhaps taking revenge for the defeat in the war or showing that the war was not yet over and the Aryan ideology not defeated. It was to be a message of hope for Germans holding on to the old dream, and we know such people exist."

Judge: "When you look at it like that, Berlin seems to have been a good choice. How did they know that Herr Brod was coming here?"

Prosecutor: "Before he travelled here, Herr Brod announced his itinerary and his programme."

Judge: "He was an old man, over 80. What if he had changed his mind at the last minute and decided not to come?"

Prosecutor: "You are right, he came here despite his health concerns. Had he not come, we believe that another Jewish intellectual in West Germany would have been targeted."

Judge: "And they sent a half-German, half-Turkish man living in Istanbul to carry out this attack?"

Prosecutor: "It seems the attacker has sentiments of personal revenge. The death of both his parents in the war . . ."

Ferdy Kaplan: "Herr Staatsanwalt . . ."

Judge: "Wait a moment, Herr Kaplan, let Herr Staatsanwalt finish. I will come to you."

Prosecutor: "We contacted the Turkish police forces. They said that Ferdy Kaplan participated in the protests against the right-wing government in 1960, but after that he was not known to be part of any active movement and had no affiliations with leftist associations. They assume that although he seemed to be living a quiet and ordinary life, he actually joined right-wing and racist groups. They will provide us with detailed information of their intelligence within a few days."

Judge: "Is it possible that the defendant has links with Palestinian militants? As we know, since Israel defeated the Arab armies last year, violence has been spreading across Europe as well as in the region. We hear of a new incident every other day."

Prosecutor: "This is something we are looking into. We have asked for information from the Israeli police on this matter."

Ferdy Kaplan: "Unrelated assumptions, irrelevant stories. Supposedly information will come from Turkish police . . . information will come from Israeli police . . . It's all utterly meaningless . . ."

Most of the bodies buried under the ruins of Berlin were never recovered. As the cries from beneath the rubble grew quiet, the smell of rotting flesh filled the air. Trapped under a shattered door, Ferdy stopped moaning and lost consciousness. When his grandfather finally found him, having searched widely for him, he could hardly recognise his grandson behind the dried blood that covered his face. He cleaned Ferdy's eyes, mouth and neck, and dripped water between his cracked lips. He lifted him onto his back and carried him to the Red Army medical base. He spoke to the soldiers there in a way they understood, managing to convince them. The medics wrapped Ferdy's head in a bandage and gave him some painkillers. They whispered to his grandfather that the boy's condition was not at all promising. His grandfather carried Ferdy back to their half-destroyed home, where he slept deliriously. For days he waited for his mother and father, dreaming that when he awoke he would find them at his side. It was a dream he had had often during the war.

Ferdy began slowly to recover. He got used to his grandfather's cooking. He read the books he found in the rubble. His grandfather became his tutor. They read together and painted together. Before long, they began to laugh together. That brought them closer. It was then that his grandfather spoke to Ferdy about a serious matter. He said that he was not a Nazi and, like many Germans, had had to hide his beliefs out of fear. He spoke of the evil of Nazism. Ferdy did not understand. He did not believe that his mother, his father, their neighbours and Hitler himself were wrong. How then could he be sure of the truth? He followed his grandfather who said, "We shall paint pictures, so we can forget and heal our wounds." With each colour, he learnt to see the beautiful soul at the heart of the ruins. He looked at the devastated buildings, but saw and painted lively houses and streets. After a year, his grandfather had another serious conversation with him. He said he was getting old and soon would not be able to look after him. He said that Ferdy should go to his father's family in Istanbul and that he would be happier living there. After all, the situation in Berlin was obvious. Ferdy cried. In agony, he set off on the journey. The longest journeys are the ones made in childhood. The life he was leaving behind was different world, one to which he could never return, and on the horizon were the clouds of a foreign sky.

"Grandpa," Ferdy said in his first letter, "I realised when

I saw Istanbul that the most beautiful city is the city without war, but still, I miss you and smoke-coated Berlin."

In response, his grandfather advised him not to neglect painting. "One begins to paint in order to forget, then one paints with the desire to remember."

In his second letter Ferdy wrote that he was having fewer headaches and was beginning to get used to Istanbul. He said he was building friendships with Jews, Christians and Muslims, and his best friend was a girl whose father was Kurdish and whose mother was Armenian. He now saw that everyone had a different colour and his grandfather's words about the race of people had started to make sense to him.

He spoke to Amalya about this and told her a story he had heard from his grandfather. Once, a writer named Franz Kafka came across a little girl who was weeping in a park. The girl had lost her doll, and Franz said to her: "I am going to look for your doll now and meet you here tomorrow." The next day he brought a letter from the doll and read it to the girl. "Please, don't be sad. I have gone on a long journey to see the world for myself. I will write to you often about what I have seen." Every day Franz brought the girl a new letter. After three weeks, he came with a doll. "Look," he said, "here is your baby doll, it came back to you." The girl was happy to see her doll was back with her, but said the doll looked different. Franz said, "Journeys always change people." Everybody had a journey like this in their lifetime. Ferdy spoke sadly. "As we were about to part, my grandfather told me this story. Now I understand him. The journey has changed me as well."

The next day Amalya met him with a book in her hand. "There was a book by your Franz Kafka at our house, I found it among my uncle's books. But it's in German, I can't understand it." Ferdy took the book, he read the first story, translating it paragraph by paragraph. They read a story every day. Sometimes they would laugh, and sometimes they would feel anxious. As they finished the book, they said, "Our Franz." They repeated it. "He is our Franz."

After Amalya went to live in France, Ferdy Kaplan faced the sorrow of discrimination on two more occasions. During the pogrom against non-Muslims in Istanbul in September 1955, which resulted in the murder of 17 people, the rape of 60 women and the looting of 5,317 homes, shops, churches and synagogues, Ferdy's German identity was remembered, too. He was beaten up in the neighbourhood square and his leg was broken. They all, including one of his friends from high school, made fun of him. They wrote his name on the wall, spelling it *Ferdi*. "Wasn't your father a Turk? Why do you spell your name with a *y*, like Germans, and not with an *i*, like Turks?" Ferdy stayed at home, bedridden for weeks. The distress grew inside him. One night he awoke with a start. He described his dream to his grandmother. "In the dream, I saw my mother. We were in a city I did not know, standing in an empty street. She came and took me in her arms. Stay with me, she said. I was still a child. I cried and said, Don't leave me, Mama." His grandmother told him this dream was a sign that he should go back to Germany, where he would be safer. Ferdy was determined to stay in Istanbul and in his neighbourhood. However, six months later, when his grandmother died, he moved to another neighbourhood. As he was moving away, he did something that had long been on his mind. He tracked down his old friend from high school who was responsible for breaking his leg. Catching him in a shadowy corner, he hit him with a stick and broke his nose. Covering his face with a mask, Ferdy vanished into the dark streets. Five years later, when Ferdy took part in anti-government protests, the images of those days were fresh in his mind. He was convinced that it was time for politics to change, for him and for everyone. He was arrested during a demonstration. The police reminded him of his father, as did his old friends from the neighbour-hood. "Your father was a nationalist, why are you acting against your nation? Or is it German blood in your veins instead of Turkish blood?" Ferdy ignored these words he had heard so often. His mind was busy with Amalya. She was leaving for Paris that same day, but Ferdy would now not be able to see her off and say goodbye.

Judge: "Herr Staatsanwalt, is there a link between this attack and the other attacks on the student leaders? Are you still considering that possibility?"

Prosecutor: "Herr Richter, we are not certain, we are still look-ing into it. This may be part of their plan to cause instability and chaos in our country. If they succeed, they will present their antiquated ideas as a new hope."

Judge: "You must find some factual evidence. Otherwise, the case will have no legal foundation."

Prosecutor: "Yes, I am aware of that. I am sure we will get some hard evidence soon."

Ferdy Kaplan: "I don't think that's possible."

Prosecutor: "Herr Kaplan, you persist with such assertions, but your confidence is groundless."

Ferdy Kaplan: "It is not as groundless as your claims. That we know."

Prosecutor: "You are forever disagreeing, yet you do not provide us with any information."

Ferdy Kaplan: "How can you say I do not provide you with information? You had no idea who the old man was. You only learnt his identity when I told you. What more do you want?"

Prosecutor: "We want to know what your purpose is. We want to know your organisation, your collaborators and your plans."

Ferdy Kaplan: "I will tell you, but again you won't understand me."

Prosecutor: "What can you tell us?"

Ferdy Kaplan: "You are searching in the wrong place. You are not even trying to look in the right place."

Prosecutor: "Where should we look, Herr Kaplan? You wounded a writer and you killed a student. Where else should we look?"

Ferdy Kaplan: "It is as if I were the one leading this hearing, not you! If I stop speaking, you will be left high and dry."

Prosecutor: "I do not agree. When you tried to run away at the scene, we apprehended you and brought you here. We found the Nazi roots in your past. We looked into your parents' connections. We obtained information about you from Istanbul. We put the case within a framework."

Ferdy Kaplan: "That framework has no foundation. If you looked at it objectively, you would understand, but you prefer to believe meaningless stories."

Prosecutor: "What is wrong with those so-called stories? During the war you were in Berlin. You were taken by your family to Nazi rallies. You grew up with that enthusiasm and pride."

Ferdy Kaplan: "These are parts of my life that have long been forgotten."

Prosecutor: "You may have forgotten, but you were reminded of them throughout your time in Istanbul. There you encountered hostility towards foreigners, you were assaulted, you were humiliated and, as a result, your faith was reawakened."

Ferdy Kaplan: "You are drawing the wrong conclusions from real events."

Prosecutor: "In my opinion, you took the wrong path due to certain events. Those events reconnected you with past memories, and now you have decided to create the future that your parents were unable to achieve."

Ferdy Kaplan: "That's enough."

Prosecutor: "When you heard the truth—"

Ferdy Kaplan: "I have not heard a single true word from you. You are trying to put your lies in my mouth."

Prosecutor: "Why are you so agitated?"

Ferdy Kaplan: "I defend the things I have done, but you are asking me to become someone I am not, you are forcing me to wear a straitjacket."

Prosecutor: "We are not forcing you to wear anything. I do not doubt your sanity for now, but you need to recognise the insanity of what you did. You are trying to revive a dead idea and a dark history."

Ferdy Kaplan: "The racism you are describing is nothing to me, merely a wound from my childhood."

Prosecutor: "What if that wound had been reopened once more?"

Ferdy Kaplan: "That wound was a big mistake, and it is buried under the rubble of history, along with my parents."

Prosecutor: "I do want to believe what you say, but it does not help to explain the chain of events."

Ferdy Kaplan: "Forget about the chain, let it go, just believe what I tell you."

Prosecutor: "Why are you before this court, then? You tell us. Go on. Why did you try to kill a Jewish writer?"

Ferdy Kaplan: "I did not try to kill a Jewish writer."

Prosecutor: "Oh, now, is this the new game you are going to play? It was only yesterday that you told us how you intended to kill Max Brod."

Ferdy Kaplan: "A man is more than his identity."

Prosecutor: "Are you talking about his Jewishness?"

Ferdy Kaplan: "I don't consider Max Brod a Jewish writer; I consider him Franz Kafka's most trusted friend. That is how I see him."

Judge: "Herr Kaplan, I hope you will answer the prosecution's allegations more clearly. I don't understand what you are saying. If you aren't racist, then what are you?"

Ferdy Kaplan: "What am I supposed to be?"

Judge: "I'm asking you, Herr Kaplan, what are you?"

Ferdy Kaplan: "I am a volunteer trying to fulfil the Will of a dead person."

Judge: "What Will? What has that to do with the attack?"

Ferdy Kaplan: "The event has nothing to do with race and religion, contrary to what you claim. I came here to kill a writer who became disloyal to his friend."

Judge: "You are saying Max Brod was disloyal? To whom?"

Ferdy Kaplan: "To Franz Kafka."

Judge: "Kafka?"

Ferdy Kaplan: "The word disloyal is not enough. He betrayed him."

Judge: "Herr Kaplan, please explain what you mean."

Ferdy Kaplan: "When Kafka died, he left a Will that asked Herr Brod to burn all his writings and manuscripts. Not satisfied with just one Will, he left two separate handwritten Wills, almost begging Herr Brod."

Judge: "And in your view this is not only disloyalty, but betrayal?"

Ferdy Kaplan: "Herr Brod ignored the Will of his best friend. Instead of burning his manuscripts, he published them one by one."

4

WEST BERLIN
PRISON

The police make inquiries in Paris and Tel Aviv and request new documents. They study the books of Max Brod and Franz Kafka. In a trial that is moving in a direction they do not understand, they are searching for evidence that will allow them to set what the defendant says in a coherent framework.

Kommissar Müller Kommissar Müller, accompanied by his officers, goes to see Ferdy Kaplan in Tegel prison. In the interview room, he places two cups of coffee on the table. He watches Ferdy Kaplan drink his coffee and occasionally turn his head to look out of the window at the courtyard.

Ferdy Kaplan: "Coffee is good for a headache."

Kommissar Müller: "Do you have a headache?"

Ferdy Kaplan: "May I have a cigarette?"

Kommissar Müller: "Here you are."

Ferdy Kaplan: "Thank you."

Kommissar Müller: "You look tired, Herr Kaplan. Are you not sleeping well?"

Ferdy Kaplan: "It is not possible to sleep. I keep returning to the same things."

Kommissar Müller: "Now, that is difficult for me to understand. You openly defend the attack, you feel proud of it, even, and then you can't sleep because of anxiety, is that it?"

Ferdy Kaplan: "It is not anxiety, it is grief. My head is full of faces and voices. The face of the dead young man, his mother's cry . . ."

Kommissar Müller: "These are things that will stay with you for ever."

Ferdy Kaplan: "And why are you so relieved? Is it because the case has been solved?"

Kommissar Müller: "The case has not yet been solved. We have only your words to go by and there are many unanswered questions."

Ferdy Kaplan: "Still, you seem relaxed."

Kommissar Müller: "Well, we are glad to hear that this attack was not motivated by anti-Semitism. This country is ready to face the death of great authors, but not for the reopening of old wounds."

Ferdy Kaplan: "When they heard what I had to say, the prosecutor and the judge sighed with relief. So, that is the reason . . ."

Kommissar Müller: "Sometimes it is not the crime itself that counts, but its objective."

Ferdy Kaplan: "In spite of this, the journalists will say that it stems from anti-Jewish motives. It is a Jewish writer from Israel that we are talking about."

Kommissar Müller: "Frankly, Herr Kaplan, we trust your

testimony. If the incident leaks to the press and unwanted comments appear, then we will release your statements."

Ferdy Kaplan: "I didn't see any journalists at the hearings. Is that right?"

Kommissar Müller: "We are keeping the case away from the press. They seem to be satisfied with the story we put out initially, that the murder was fuelled by jealousy. That is why we are withholding the name of Max Brod. This is also Herr Brod's wish: he does not want to be pestered by journalists."

Ferdy Kaplan: "So, why are you here?"

Kommissar Müller: "We wanted to pay a private visit to you."

Ferdy Kaplan: "So far as I know, according to the law, once the trial begins the police are no longer in charge of the case, is that right?"

Kommissar Müller: "We wanted to make an off-the-record visit."

Ferdy Kaplan: "You are holding me in this prison. Is that also off the record? Only convicted felons are held here. Prisoners like me, whose trials are ongoing, are not held here. Why am I here?"

Kommissar Müller: "It is a security measure. We have no knowledge of the kind of organisation behind you and its capacity. We thought it better to keep you in a more secure place."

Ferdy Kaplan: "And is it another of your precautionary measures to have police escorts for the prison officers who take me from prison to the courtroom?"

Kommissar Müller: "Yes, that is the precise reason. It is for security that we accompany you during your transfer."

Ferdy Kaplan: "You say that you uphold the law against me, yet you are breaching the law at every turn."

Kommissar Müller: "Had you helped us by being more cooperative, no doubt we would have acted differently."

Ferdy Kaplan: "You don't need to take such measures on my behalf, Herr Müller. I'm not such an important person."

Kommissar Müller: "If only I could believe you. We know your identity, Herr Kaplan, but we don't know who you really are. We are trying to navigate our way in the dark."

Ferdy Kaplan: "So you are here in the hope of shining some light on the situation, is that so?"

Kommissar Müller: "I have some questions to put to you. That is why I wanted to talk to you."

Ferdy Kaplan: "Fine. That is not a problem for me. I am listening to you."

Kommissar Müller: "Let us speak freely. This conversation will not be recorded, so we can clarify everything that is uncertain. We need convincing information and a clear motive. And the details that do not need to go into your official statement . . ."

Ferdy Kaplan: "And you expect me to collaborate with you?"

Kommissar Müller: "Do not misunderstand me. I don't want names. I won't even ask you about the woman who was with you during the attack. You can keep that to yourself."

Ferdy Kaplan: "So what do you want then?"

Kommissar Müller: "If you can point us in the right direction and stop us from going down the wrong path, that's enough."

Ferdy Kaplan: "Herr Staatsanwalt refused to do that when I suggested it at the hearing."

Kommissar Müller: "I will not reject it. I shall pay attention to the direction in which you take us."

Ferdy Kaplan: "Why should I do this?"

Kommissar Müller: "If you help us, then we will help you. We will make sure you get a reduced sentence from the court."

Ferdy Kaplan: "I am not that kind of person. You should have realised that by now."

Kommissar Müller: "There is no doubt about that. You don't have to disclose anything, but what's the harm in a little talk? Look, we have already started. [*Kommissar Müller takes two cigarettes out of his pack and offers one to Ferdy Kaplan.*] Here, have another one."

Ferdy Kaplan: "You are very generous today."

Kommissar Müller: "If the reason for the incident is as you say – that the attack was intended to punish Herr Brod for disregarding Kafka's Will and publishing his works – then the case may well be closed. But, Herr Kaplan, if there are plans to target other writers, we really need to know."

Ferdy Kaplan: "Is that your concern? There is no need for that. Herr Brod is my only target."

Kommissar Müller: "What about the others? Are the others planning to harm any writers?"

Ferdy Kaplan: "What others?"

Kommissar Müller: "People involved with *Stylo Noir* magazine."

Ferdy Kaplan: "*Stylo Noir*?"

Kommissar Müller: "Yes."

Ferdy Kaplan: "You have managed to surprise me, Herr Müller, for the first time! Have you been reading that magazine?"

Kommissar Müller: "Yes, I started reading it yesterday."

Ferdy Kaplan: "Do you know French?"

Kommissar Müller: "I lived in France when I was young. My wife is French."

Ferdy Kaplan: "Oh, is that so? In that case, please give my best regards to your wife."

Kommissar Müller: "We have uncovered some new information. We know that the argument over Kafka began in *Stylo Noir* magazine. We would like to discuss this with you and – how shall I put it? – we would like to broaden our literary horizons a little. [*Kommissar Müller laughs and the three police officers sitting at the next table follow suit.*] In fact, I know Kafka from the books my wife reads, but I had never heard of Max Brod. Now, thanks to you, I am reading both Kafka and Brod. I understand that they were very close friends. Shall I tell you what I think?"

Ferdy Kaplan: "Yes, please."

Kommissar Müller: "I think Herr Brod acted correctly. Personally, I would not have expected Herr Brod to agree when Kafka wanted him to burn all his works. A good friend is someone who despite you – despite your mistakes, I mean – does the right thing by you. Otherwise he is not a friend but a servant following in your trail."

Ferdy Kaplan: "Satan, too, was of that opinion."

Kommissar Müller: "Satan?"

Ferdy Kaplan: "When God created man in his own image, Satan objected. His objection was that it would destroy God's uniqueness and that God's inimitability would be lost. Satan disobeyed God purely to protect God. It is like

Herr Brod disobeying Kafka in order to protect Kafka."

Kommissar Müller: "That is interesting."

Ferdy Kaplan: "People like him deserve Dante's *Inferno*."

Kommissar Müller: "That is even more interesting."

Ferdy Kaplan: "Are you going to keep repeating the same word: interesting?"

Kommissar Müller: "You are comparing Herr Brod to Satan, who disobeyed God. So, you are obeying God's will – or, rather, trying to fulfil his will – by punishing Herr Brod. Is that so?"

Ferdy Kaplan: "You may see it like that if you wish . . ."

Kommissar Müller: [*Kommissar Müller holds a copy of the magazine in front of him.*] "I will use this word again and say that this coincidence is most interesting. I read an article last night in an old issue of *Stylo Noir*. It explores the idea that it is free will that brings man closer to God. Aha, here it is! 'Kafka's Wishes' is the title of the article. Or perhaps I should interpret it as 'Kafka's Will'? The author of the article uses a pen name, no doubt. Could you by any chance be the author, Herr Kaplan?"

Ferdy Kaplan: "You really have done your homework, Herr Müller, but I am not the author of that piece."

Kommissar Müller: "Look, written here are the words you used. The words God, Satan, Kafka and Brod are repeated over and over. Even Dante is here . . ."

Ferdy Kaplan: "I read that article when it was published. It did a good job of explaining the confusion between right and wrong. Satan falls into wrongdoing in his search for the right thing."

Kommissar Müller: "Or, by going in the wrong direction, Satan ends up achieving the right result."

Ferdy Kaplan: "One could think that way . . ."

Kommissar Müller: "As you know, *Stylo Noir* means black pen; most of the writers here use pseudonyms to hide their identities in the dark shadow of their pens. The magazine attracted attention through its Kafka debate rather than its anonymous authors. [*Kommissar Müller takes a file out of his bag.*] Here, the French police sent us some photographs. They believe that some of them may be contributors to *Stylo Noir* magazine. Have a look."

[*Ferdy Kaplan glances at the photographs.*]

Ferdy Kaplan: "Well, my photograph is not here."

Kommissar Müller: "Did you notice the photographs of the women?"

Ferdy Kaplan: "No. Why would I?"

Kommissar Müller: "They all have short hair."

Ferdy Kaplan: "Do you think that is significant?"

Kommissar Müller: "Yes, it has a meaning, but it has nothing to do with the case."

Ferdy Kaplan: "Well, I wonder . . ."

Kommissar Müller: "You know the movie 'À bout de souffle', don't you? Since that movie, French women have changed. The leading actress, Jean Seberg, inspired everyone to have their hair cut short like hers. Look, the women in these photographs are mirror images of her."

Ferdy Kaplan: "A strange hypothesis."

Kommissar Müller: "Our German women do not have such

a movie. I mean, they do not have an idol who can attract the attention of young people."

Ferdy Kaplan: "Maybe they have one, but men can't see it. No, let me correct that: the police can't see it."

[*Ferdy Kaplan laughs for the first time.*]

Amalya was heavy-hearted when she returned to Paris. It was as if she could not hear her mother, and was not aware of the presence of her mother's partner, Dr Hugo. She took no part in their conversations. In the evenings, she retreated to her room and ate her meals alone. One day, when they went out to see a movie at her mother's insistence, she said to her: "Eliz, when I wrote to you, I told you that if you wanted to die happy, you should never set eyes on the new face of Istanbul. Well, the same applies to me: I will not see it again. I will keep hold of the old Istanbul that I know and store its love in my heart."

Amalya opened her suitcase a few days later. She took out the picture Ferdy had drawn and hung it above her desk. Her mother and Dr Hugo came in and looked at the picture.

"Dr Hugo," Amalya said, "you have good taste and a knowledge of art. Tell me what you think of this picture."

Dr Hugo looked closely at it. "I must say, I have never before seen such pencil use or perspective. Who is the artist?"

"A friend of mine in Istanbul drew it."

Dr Hugo stepped back and examined it from a distance. "This is a friend who views you and Istanbul in a unique way. The woman in the picture is clearly you, but the look he has drawn on your face is one I have never seen. It is impressive."

"If you say so, then it must be true," Amalya said, fixing her eyes on the picture.

Amalya began to drink heavily to rid herself of the thoughts gathering in her head. She would hang around the dark streets in the heart of the Latin Quarter and come home late at night. Thinking it might do her good, Dr Hugo introduced her to the young people who published *Stylo Noir* magazine. The magazine was very popular with students. It asked, "Should Kafka be burned?", which set off a debate in school canteens and dimly lit bars. The magazine announced the results of the survey on its centre pages: "Kafka should be burned!" A letter to the magazine from a reader stated: "Kafka can no longer be erased, but Max Brod, who was unfaithful to him, may pay the price." Then the magazine asked its readers: "Should Max Brod pay the price?" Canteens and bars witnessed more heated debates. The result of the survey appeared this time on the cover of the magazine, with a black and white photograph: "Max Brod must pay the price!"

Amalya took part in the debates, sold *Stylo Noir* in the canteens, sometimes stayed overnight at the magazine's office, but she still could not get Istanbul out of her mind. She wandered around like a drunk, even when she had not had a drop of alcohol.

Eliz spoke to Dr Hugo about her. "I have tried everything. There is nothing more I can do. Tell me, what do you think I should do?"

Dr Hugo suggested the three of them take a trip and leave the city for a few days.

"Where to?" Eliz asked.

"We will visit my village," Dr Hugo said. They left Paris in the early hours the following morning and headed south. They drove for six hours – with stops for rest and refreshment – through the autumnal countryside. When they reached the village of Oradour-sur-Glane, they checked into the hotel, then went out to have a look around. Dr Hugo told them that there no members of his family left in the village and that this was the second time he had come here since the war. When he passed the church, he came across an old woman. He hugged the woman, said a few words to her and walked on. "That woman was my mother's friend," he said. He looked at the surrounding buildings and colourful walls, rubbing his eyes.

Eliz asked him, "Are you alright, my dear?"

Dr Hugo smiled and said, "You know, I was born in this village, but this is not the village where I was born."

Eliz stared at him. "What does that mean? You have brought us to your village and are speaking in riddles. You look confused, as if you, not we, were the stranger here."

After strolling through a few streets, they crossed to the other side of the main road. Dr Hugo pointed to the ruins ahead: "There is the village where I was born." Among the trees were abandoned old houses. Partially collapsed walls. Fragments of bricks. Burnt cars.

"During the war I was not in this area, but in Paris," he explained. "The Normandy landings had just begun. Attacks against the Germans and their collaborators increased from all sides. Here the Resistance managed to capture an S.S. officer by the name of Helmut Kämpfe. No ordinary officer, he was one of the few commanders to have worn the most important medals awarded by the Nazis, and he was a favourite of Hitler. Two members of the French Militia told the Germans that the officer was being held in the village of Oradour-sur-Glane. The intelligence was incorrect. The Resistance had killed Helmut Kämpfe as soon as they captured him and had immediately left the area. The forces of the 2nd S.S. Panzer Division Das Reich surrounded the village, but could not find any trace of the officer, so they decided to punish the villagers. It was the fifth day of the Normandy landings, and they were full of rage. They herded the women and children into the church. They locked the men in the barns. First, they turned their machine guns on the barns. They shot the men in the legs and while the men were lying on the ground, wounded, they poured petrol on them and set fire to them. Next, they went to the church. They placed explosives by the wall, causing panic. The women and children threw themselves at the doors and windows, trying to escape, but none of them got away. They were met with the merciless fire of machine guns. That night, the German army looted and burned all the houses. I have memorised the numbers: 247 women, 205 children and 190 men were killed. Among them were my mother, my father and my sister. When the war ended, it was decided that the village should be left as it was and a new one built on the other side of the road. I came to help with the construction of the new village. I worked for a few months, then left. This is the first time since then that I have been back."

Dr Hugo showed them the corner covered with grass and rocks where his house had once stood. He walked from one end of the cemetery to the other without speaking, then turned back to the new village. With Eliz on one side and Amalya on the other, he walked up and down the streets of the new village until the sky grew dark. A few times he greeted people he knew and told Eliz and Amalya their stories.

"Those responsible," he said, "were punished for their deeds, not only the Germans but their French collaborators too. French Militia leader Joseph Darnand, a vile murderer, was captured in Italy, whither he had fled. He was tried and executed by firing squad. But two militiamen targeted this village, and one, after all this time, has still not been caught. My friends from the old Resistance group are on his trail. They recently discovered that he is living in Paris under a false identity. It is only a matter of time; he will be apprehended before long."

They had dinner at the restaurant next to the hotel. Eliz held Dr Hugo's hand. "Now I understand why you have never wanted to talk about your past. I wish you had brought us here sooner," she said.

"You are right," the doctor said. "I brought you here so that Amalya might breathe the fresh air of a different environment, but this trip has been good for me, too. It is not only the faces of my loved ones that have lived in my mind for years, but also the ruined houses and graves. They come with me everywhere."

Amalya took Dr Hugo's other hand. "I know you take care of me, and I am very grateful for it. I want you not to worry about me anymore. I'll be better from now on."

Kommissar Müller: "Would you have wanted to meet Herr Brod?"
Ferdy Kaplan: "You cannot know how much I wanted to meet him."

Kommissar Müller: "I have news for you. Herr Brod will be attending the hearing."

Ferdy Kaplan: "Well, this news is something to be happy about. There are matters I want to discuss with him. And I will have a chance to tell him how much I love his books."

Kommissar Müller: "Love them?"

Ferdy Kaplan: "Do not think that I despise him. I esteem him and I admire his literature. Religions, you know, have lists of 'Deadly Sins'. If there were deadly sins in literature, Herr Brod has committed one of them, more's the pity. He crushed the soul of a fellow writer by disregarding his Will."

Kommissar Müller: "I cannot understand you, no matter how hard I try."

Ferdy Kaplan: "Let me put it this way. If Kafka were alive today, what would he do? He would burn all his manuscripts and continue to love his friend, Brod. I, too, love Brod, but at the same time I defend the terms of Franz Kafka's Will."

Kommissar Müller: "You mentioned a list of 'Deadly Sins' in literature. Who else do you consider a sinner?"

Ferdy Kaplan: "Mine is a one-man list. There is nobody else, I assure you."

Kommissar Müller: "I find it hard to believe you, Herr Kaplan. Although your words and your tone are convincing, these old issues of *Stylo Noir* still confuse me. Look, one issue three years ago praises the Watts Riots of the black community in Los Angeles."

Ferdy Kaplan: "The people wanted to assert their right to equality, they wanted an end to racist oppression. What is wrong with that?"

Kommissar Müller: "Is this the way to protect rights? More than 30 people died."

Ferdy Kaplan: "You know that it was the police who killed all of them. It is amazing how a Berlin police officer is defending the Los Angeles police. Is that what you call police solidarity?"

Kommissar Müller: "I don't defend the police there. I believe that riots and violence are the wrong way."

Ferdy Kaplan: "Who caused that to happen? Those who died there were innocent. And tell me, what does this matter have to do with me?"

Kommissar Müller: "When I see that death is easily justified, I become suspicious. You divide the dead into the innocent and the guilty. In this way you rationalise killing and coolly go after an old man like Max Brod."

Ferdy Kaplan: "Ah, Kommissar Müller, are you aware of where we are now? This is a prison and its history is full of the brutality of the state against the people; cruelty is not limited to the Nazi era. And you, as a public servant, are talking to me about the death of innocent people. If you smell these walls – try it – you will smell the rotting lives of innocent people."

Kommissar Müller: "There is some truth in your words, I cannot deny that. But we both know you are not one of those innocent people you speak of."

Ferdy Kaplan: "Forget me, I am not important. Tell me about Herr Brod. He must be feeling better if he is able to attend court."

Kommissar Müller: "Yes, I saw him yesterday, his wound is not of great concern. He was shot in the shoulder. The doctors said he should lead a normal and comfortable life again."

Ferdy Kaplan: "That is good news."

Kommissar Müller: "Good news? Are you sure about that?"

Ferdy Kaplan: "I don't think you will understand, even if I try to explain."

Kommissar Müller: "Had you seen Herr Brod before? Before the day of the attack, I mean."

Ferdy Kaplan: "No."

Kommissar Müller: "Herr Brod said he would attend the hearing with his assistant. He turned down the offer of a police escort. He is a brave man. I will send a team to accompany him anyway. I don't want anything unfortunate to happen to him again. The woman with the short hair is still at liberty, you know."

Ferdy Kaplan: "Don't worry, nothing more will happen to Herr Brod. Some traditions are sacred. In the past, if the rope broke when a man was being hanged, it was seen as though life had smiled upon him. And he would be pardoned. I hold fast to this tradition. Herr Brod's rope broke and now he is free."

Kommissar Müller: "The writings in *Stylo Noir* are full of such weird references. Ancient times, traditions, revolutions, religions, retributions . . . It is not possible to say whether the publishers of this magazine are anarchists, communists, nihilists or simply lunatics . . ."

Ferdy Kaplan: "They are not lunatics, that is for sure. I can tell you that."

Kommissar Müller: "If only I could believe you, Herr Kaplan."

Ferdy Kaplan: "Do believe me, Herr Müller."

Kommissar Müller: "And there is something else. Something you and I have in common."

Ferdy Kaplan: "What is that?"

Kommissar Müller: "The women you and I love have the same hairstyle. My wife used to have long hair, but, like all French women, she now cuts it short."

Ferdy Kaplan: "Do you like it that way?"

Kommissar Müller: "Yes, I like it. And you?"

Ferdy Kaplan: "Herr Müller, I believe I made a mistake at the outset. I underestimated your intelligence."

5

WEST BERLIN
COURTROOM

Max Brod leaves Berlin without informing the authorities of his departure. In a letter to the court, he apologises for not attending the hearing.

"I am an old man. All this turmoil is too much for me. I am going home. My home is also Kafka's home. He and I, we completed one another. He feared death because he could not live as he pleased. Because of this, I lived life on his behalf too. Kafka left me two notes asking that all his works be burned. He had always shied away from publishing his work. One or two of his works were published as a result of my encouragement. His Will was like that of a lover who goes away saying 'Forget me', and yet has no desire ever to be forgotten. I knew it. At the beginning I had the eternal happiness of having published Kafka's works, so they saw the light of day. As I grew older, the joy in my heart started to dull and be replaced by unhappiness. I began to liken myself to Satan. Satan, who disobeyed God with the sole intention of defending God. Kafka was my God and I disregarded his Will. If Dante were alive today, he would have found me deserving of the Inferno in his *Comedy*. [*While this part of the letter is being read, Ferdy Kaplan turns and looks at Kommissar Müller, who is sitting in the row on his right. Kommissar Müller likewise turns his head towards him.*] Herr Richter, had I come to court and been present, I would not have been able to assist you. I did not see the attackers. I cannot identify them. Whoever they are, I forgive them. I only wish they had been a little more careful and sent an old man like me to the other world instead of an innocent young student. That would have pleased me."

Prosecutor: "Herr Kaplan, did you intend to murder this kind of man?"

Ferdy Kaplan: "Well, to be honest, I hadn't even considered the idea that Herr Brod might feel the slightest remorse towards Kafka."

Prosecutor: "He is a man who has done good both to Kafka and to literature itself."

Ferdy Kaplan: "I wouldn't go so far as that."

Prosecutor: "Why not?"

Ferdy Kaplan: "Herr Brod published the manuscripts in his possession by altering and editing them. It is not known where he found the authority or the right to do this. Altering a text means ruining it."

Prosecutor: "On what basis do you say this?"

Ferdy Kaplan: "Let me give you an example. Kafka wrote a novel that he called *The Man Who Disappeared*. Herr Brod published it under the title *Amerika*. Even the title was changed, so, how can we know how much of the content of this book really belongs to Kafka?"

Prosecutor: "Perhaps that is an appropriate change to make."

Ferdy Kaplan: "Is it appropriate for Kafka or Brod? For instance, Kafka liked long paragraphs, yet Brod cut them up and shortened the sentences. For whom is this appropriate?"

Prosecutor: "I was speaking generally. I cannot comment as I haven't read the book."

Ferdy Kaplan: "Have you read any Kafka?"

Prosecutor: "I have read only one of his books. Now, because of the developments in this case, I have bought some of his books and hope to read them."

Ferdy Kaplan: "Which book did you read?"

Prosecutor: "*The Metamorphosis*. You know, a man who transforms into an insect . . ."

Ferdy Kaplan: "Do you remember the cover of the book? What was the picture on it?"

Prosecutor: "I think . . . there was a gloomy-looking room . . . a huge insect hidden under the bed. Well, the cover was like the story itself."

Ferdy Kaplan: "Exactly. Poor Kafka. He knew from the very beginning that his books were going to be treated unfairly. He anticipated it. He himself sent *The Metamorphosis* to the publisher. Then he wrote a letter to the publisher, requesting them not to put a picture of an insect on the cover. He stressed that no insect should appear on the cover, not even in the background. The original publisher did as Kafka requested, but what happened after that? Fifty years have gone by and now, if you look at any cover, published anywhere in the world, it is scarcely possible to find one without an insect. Is that the way to understand and be loyal to Kafka?"

Prosecutor: "You are exaggerating, Herr Kaplan. Regardless of the comments and the opinions, the readers understand these books and they pour their own feelings into these stories."

Ferdy Kaplan: "What Kafka left behind were the writings he kept for himself. Perhaps none of them were fully formed, perhaps he would have changed them, made some longer, some shorter. Maybe Kafka was still working on those changes, struggling with them."

Prosecutor: "Whether they were missing something, or were yet rough drafts, why should it be bad to read these texts after the death of the author and accept them in the state in which they were left?"

Ferdy Kaplan: "If the author had not expressed his wishes, then what you say would make sense. But Kafka made his wishes clear before he died and did so unambiguously."

Prosecutor: "If, for the sake of argument, we accept your point of view, it still does not justify your intention to kill. Just because someone has erred, and let's assume Max Brod was wrong in what he did, it does not mean that he deserves to die."

Ferdy Kaplan: "Herr Staatsanwalt, in my opinion we are indebted to Kafka. I believe in the eternity of the human soul and in a person's free will. If someone disregards the eternity that is Kafka's wish, then he should bear the punishment. The letter he sent to the court makes clear that Herr Brod himself expected this punishment."

Prosecutor: "If Kafka is recognised as an important person, it is because of his writing. His name would mean nothing had he written nothing. All this was made possible by Max Brod. Thanks to Brod, we know of the man Kafka. Why should we condemn Kafka to the realm of absence and nothingness, when he has already reached the realm of eternity through his writing?"

Ferdy Kaplan: "No matter how much Brod tampered with Kafka's works, he could not diminish the magic of Kafka's pen. Because Kafka had power. If there is such a person as Kafka today, it is not due to Max Brod, but despite him."

Prosecutor: "If Kafka truly wanted his works to be burned, why didn't he burn them himself? He wrote continually for many years, creating an entire body of work, and did not attempt to destroy a single piece."

Ferdy Kaplan: "We cannot be sure of that. Perhaps his works were not complete. Perhaps he wanted them to be published under his own supervision. As his illness progressed, he realised this would not be possible, yet he did not have the strength to destroy his own works. So he left himself in the hands of his most trusted friend."

Prosecutor: "This is all speculation. No judgment can be based on this, and even if it were possible, it does not warrant pursuing and murdering people. There is another way: to criticise people. I believe there have been people in the world of literature who have written about Herr Brod and criticised him, is that right?"

Ferdy Kaplan: "Yes indeed. I have read many such criticisms."

Prosecutor: "If only you had been satisfied with criticism, too."

Ferdy Kaplan: "You see Kafka as a literary treasure; like everybody else, you are content to value this treasure. But Kafka himself, as he approached the end of his life, no longer wished to identify himself as a writer. He was merely a person, and that was all. I respect that person and his right to anonymity; I respect his choice to leave this world as he wished. That is what Herr Brod ignored."

Prosecutor: "A person nearing death is like a foolish child. A child will want to touch the fire, so we intervene to prevent it. If a person who is about to die wants to throw his books into the fire, we step in to prevent him."

Ferdy Kaplan: "What is the right thing to do? Who decides that?"

Prosecutor: "There are very faithful readers of Kafka; let us leave it to them. They will protect Kafka."

Ferdy Kaplan: "Protect? He had three sisters, all of them killed in the concentration camps. Who protected them?"

Prosecutor: "That is a different question."

Ferdy Kaplan: "No, that is the real question. Had Kafka lived a little longer, he would have found himself in a concentration camp. Nobody would have protected him, just as there is nobody to protect him today."

Prosecutor: "History, our history, is full of mistakes. To prevent these mistakes recurring, we defend justice. We are defending Kafka here."

Ferdy Kaplan: "If you were committed to defending justice itself, you would not be sitting behind that desk; you would be here, in my place. No, you are not on Kafka's side, but, rather, on the side of his books. Just like Max Brod. Brod quickly forgot Kafka and loved only his written works. Only as he grew older did he realise his mistake. When his love for Kafka as a person was rekindled years later, he felt that his deeds were those of a devil. Then he felt remorse. Did you know that Brod was also once an accomplished musician? He composed music and sang opera. In recent years, he has returned to his love of music and distanced himself from literature. Although the remorse in his soul led him back to music, he could not achieve peace of mind. He longed for death."

Prosecutor: "This is your interpretation, Herr Kaplan. You are presenting your interpretation as if it were the wish of Max Brod."

Ferdy Kaplan: "Do you know how Kafka died? On his last night, he was in agony in a sanatorium. He asked the doctor to put an end to his life. When the doctor refused, Kafka screamed, 'Kill me! If you don't kill me, you are a murderer.' And now, Max Brod's soul is in agony, and he wishes us to kill him. If we don't follow his request and kill him, then we are considered murderers. This is evident from what he wrote. His letter is short but eminently clear."

Prosecutor: "You are drawing a long conclusion from a short letter."

Ferdy Kaplan: "Herr Staatsanwalt, I believe in drawing long conclusions from short letters."

Prosecutor: "Again, obscure words that are difficult to understand."

Ferdy Kaplan: "The distance between your chair and mine is so great that it is very hard for us to understand one another."

"Dear Amalya, I am writing you this postcard with a delay of six months and one week. Had I written any sooner, I would not have been able to say the words I want to say here. I could not come to the airport to say goodbye to you because I was under arrest. In custody, my German identity proved both a reason for my humiliation by the police and also an advantage. The others who were arrested with me at the protest remained in custody for a week, but the police were not happy to see the German passport in my pocket, so they released me after two days. How could I write to you, then? Although I loved you, I had to hide it from you and from myself. To do otherwise would have been unfair to my fiancée and disloyal to the life we had dreamt of together. So, I believed in the power of time and thought that I could bear your absence, but, eventually, I was defeated by time. Last week, without realising it, I called my fiancée by your name. Who is Amalya? she asked. What do you mean? I responded. You just called me Amalya, she said. Really? Yes, really. After six months, I became helpless. I told her everything. We bowed our heads. We said farewell and separated. I have been wandering aimlessly for a week, and I don't know what to do. And now, on the back of a postcard on which I've drawn a view of Istanbul, I'm writing to tell you that I love you. Amalya! I believe in myself, in you, and in time."

It was a postcard covered in fine sketches that showed the view of a seagull as it flew over the Maiden's Tower and, behind it, the Bosphorus stretching out like a snake. The seagull was gliding with its wings outstretched, suspended by the north-easterly wind. Amalya felt as though she were floating alongside the seagull, looking down and watching the people strolling on the shore. A ferry was crossing the Bosphorus, ploughing through the waves. Amalya followed the ferry, dived into the wind and descended to the rear deck. There she found Ferdy watching the sea. The sun was setting over Istanbul.

Amalya dipped down towards Ferdy, her mouth close to his, and she inhaled his breath with a feeling of melancholy. At that moment, her mother entered the room. Amalya placed the card on the table and turned to her mother. She told her about the beauty of old times and how she missed Istanbul. "Is it only Istanbul that you miss?" her mother said. "No, not only that." "Go then, my dear. Go and do what you have to do." Amalya smiled like a mischievous child and said, "I have a better idea."

Prosecutor: "Herr Richter! The argument about defending Kafka's last Will, about avenging him, no less, was not the defendant's own idea. As we have established, this topic has been a matter of discussion in magazines in France for some twenty years."

Judge: "How, were they speaking openly of revenge?"

Prosecutor: "Articles with such arguments were published, yes."

Judge: "I assume that you have some evidence to present."

Prosecutor: "We have some publications at hand. The issue was raised in *Axiome*, a magazine that ceased publication twenty years ago. Recently, *Stylo Noir*, a magazine popular among young people, has covered this topic more frequently and in a sharper way."

Judge: "What sort of magazines are they? Are they publications of underground groups?"

Prosecutor: "*Axiome* was an underground publication put out by the French Resistance during the Second World War. After the war, the magazine was published openly and continued until 1948. In several issues it featured debates on the topic 'Should Kafka be burned?' and ran a survey on this."

Ferdy Kaplan: "Herr Staatsanwalt, are you trying to connect me with a debate that took place when I was a child?"

Prosecutor: "We are trying to get to the bottom of this idea you expound and to determine the organisation you are involved with."

Judge: "Herr Kaplan, you may speak when it is your turn, but for the moment you must remain silent."

Ferdy Kaplan: "Well, I am listening. Let us see where you are heading."

Judge: "Herr Staatsanwalt, you say that *Axiome* magazine was published by the Resistance. There were political issues to engage with during the war; why would they turn their attention to literary matters?"

Prosecutor: "From the very beginning, the magazine carried articles on art and culture. By weaving a thread of resistance through this field, it was able to maintain its political affiliations, too."

Judge: "It would seem from your comments that *Axiome* magazine encouraged violence against certain writers. Is that so?"

Prosecutor: "I would say that applies more to *Stylo Noir*."

Judge: "Who publishes this magazine? The same members of the Resistance?"

Prosecutor: "No. A group of young people studying at different universities began publishing *Stylo Noir* ten years ago. It constantly reinvents itself with new contributors."

Judge: "Are these young people following in the footsteps of the previous generation?"

Prosecutor: "It appears that *Stylo Noir* inherited the idea of defending Kafka and his Will from *Axiome*. Of course, *Stylo Noir* went further and called for Max Brod to be punished."

Judge: "By punish, what do they mean? Do they mean murder?"

Prosecutor: "Not in so many words. They say that Max Brod should pay the price, they have published pieces about that, but they don't specify what they mean by 'pay the price'."

Judge: "It's a flexible expression, it can be taken in many ways."

Prosecutor: "Despite the ambiguity of the word 'price', some comments indicate a particular direction. I can cite some of the words they use to describe Herr Brod. [*The prosecutor holds up a paper and reads from it.*] Unfaithful is what they call him, vile and wretched. They say he is more treacherous than the traitors in the war."

Judge: "Those are dangerous words. We know that during the war, traitors were sentenced to death."

Prosecutor: "Articles and letters along those lines were published in the magazine."

Judge: "Did none of this arouse the attention of the authorities?"

Prosecutor: "*Stylo Noir* is the kind of magazine that uses satirical language, publishes caricatures and is often humorous about serious subjects. Because it wasn't clear when they were being serious and when they were being humorous, they did not attract attention."

Judge: "Is it possible that the former publishers of *Axiome* have some ties with the young people who publish *Stylo Noir* and have led them in a certain direction?"

Prosecutor: "These are people from whom anything may be expected. For instance, one member of the *Axiome* group appeared somewhere else. Seven years ago, a plane was hijacked in Portugal and as it flew over Lisbon anti-government flyers were dropped all over the city. The hijackers then landed the plane in Morocco. One of those hijackers was a Resistance fighter who had published *Axiome* magazine. We believe that these people are able to influence the editorial team at *Stylo Noir* magazine."

Judge: "Very well. What is the nature of Ferdy Kaplan's affiliation with *Stylo Noir*?"

Prosecutor: "We are awaiting a new intelligence report from France. The defendant is not cooperating with us."

Ferdy Kaplan: "Herr Richter, I have given both the prosecutor and the police very clear answers on this matter. *Stylo Noir* is a magazine that is available all over Paris. Like many other people, I buy it and read it. I have no other affiliation with the magazine."

Judge: "Where did this idea come from, the idea for an attack on Max Brod, and avenging Kafka? Is it something you came up with yourself?"

Ferdy Kaplan: "Yes. I have been a fervent reader of Kafka for a great many years. Beyond his writings, I love and respect him as a person. I am mature enough to make my own decisions. I was not in need of anyone's order to carry out this mission."

Judge: "You shoot people and then you boast about it, as you are doing now."

Prosecutor: "Herr Richter, the defendant has a habit of speaking in an unorthodox way. Even when he gives us useful information, he still prevents us from reaching any conclusion. He painted a picture for us and gave us a frame, but never mentioned what was behind it. For this reason, it is possible that the French magazines are an instrument to manipulate us. Perhaps there is another network involved, such as a foreign intelligence service."

Judge: "Are you referring to East Germany? Are you still considering that as an option?"

Prosecutor: "The murder of a Jewish writer in the West could serve the interest of East Germany, as it would put the burden of the past back on this side. We are investigating this."

Ferdy Kaplan: "That is a waste of time, Herr Staatsanwalt, it really is."

Prosecutor: "When you are so insistent, it makes us suspicious and we envisage the opposite of what you say."

Ferdy Kaplan: "From the beginning you have doubted everything I have said, and you have described me by all sorts of names. You have called me an anarchist, you have called me a lunatic. And now you add spy for East Germany to the list . . . What sort of list is it?"

Prosecutor: "Herr Kaplan, there is something else I would like to ask you. Had you succeeded in killing Herr Brod, would you have moved on to another target? What would you have done next?"

Ferdy Kaplan: "I know exactly what I would have done: I

would have written a letter to Herr Brod. You may wonder what use it is to write a letter to a dead man. Well, Kafka wrote a letter to his living father, he poured his heart into the pages, but he never gave the letter to his father. This more than anything reveals the nature of Kafka's soul. Not every piece of writing is meant for publication. Kafka shared that letter with his mother and sisters, but never with the one to whom it was addressed: his father. He wrote the letter primarily for himself, for his past, for his weakness and for his disappointments. And what happened upon Kafka's death? The 45-page letter he wrote to his father was turned into a book and published along with his other works all over the world, as *Letter to His Father*. This is what hurts the human soul."

6

WEST BERLIN
PRISON

The next morning Kommissar Müller comes to the prison, just as the first sunbeams fall on the windows. He and Ferdy Kaplan sit at a table, facing one another. The chirps of the birds outside can be heard. When the birds stop chirping, the room falls silent. They sip their coffee. With tired eyes they look at each other.

Kommissar Müller: "Still having difficulty sleeping, Herr Kaplan? You look tired . . ."

Ferdy Kaplan: "I can see that you have not been sleeping well, either."

[*Ferdy Kaplan looks at Kommissar Müller and then to the police officers standing beside him.*]

Kommissar Müller: "We are dealing with matters that keep us from our sleep. We spent the night on our feet. You could have slept. I would have thought you would be used to living here by now."

Ferdy Kaplan: "I am settling in, don't you worry. Were you following new lines of enquiry?"

Kommissar Müller: "As you know, we are constantly chasing new things . . ."

Ferdy Kaplan: "So what brings you here at this time of the morning?"

Kommissar Müller: "You have a hearing, Herr Kaplan, or did you forget about that? We are here to take you to the courthouse."

Ferdy Kaplan: "I asked what brought you here so early. The hearing is in the afternoon, yet you are here at dawn. Are you wanting to have another conversation with me off the record?"

Kommissar Müller: "That is what we need."

Ferdy Kaplan: "Are you confused again?"

Kommissar Müller: "The threads in my mind have become a little tangled, so I have come to ask for your help."

Ferdy Kaplan: "I hope you're not going to ask me the same old questions."

Kommissar Müller: "Not old ones. I have new questions."

Ferdy Kaplan: "New evidence . . ."

Kommissar Müller: "No new evidence at all. It was during the hearing yesterday that I lost hold of the threads and felt as if I was in a daze."

Ferdy Kaplan: "About what? Many things were discussed yesterday."

Kommissar Müller: "About the things Herr Brod said in his letter . . ."

Ferdy Kaplan: "Oh, I see, God and Satan, and so on . . . Is that what you mean?"

Kommissar Müller: "Yes, those words . . . When the letter was being read out, I noticed that you were surprised, too."

Ferdy Kaplan: "How could I not have been surprised? They were phrases that I used in my exchanges with you. For a moment I thought that the letter was fictitious, that you had written those words."

Kommissar Müller: "Are you serious? The tiredness on your face conceals your expression, Herr Kaplan. I don't understand you."

Ferdy Kaplan: "It was a fleeting thought. I knew it was improbable, so I wiped it from my mind."

Kommissar Müller: "I had no knowledge of that letter. I learnt of it at the same time as you did, at the hearing."

Ferdy Kaplan: "Well, what did you think of it when you heard its contents?"

Kommissar Müller: "I was so surprised that I could not think of anything at first."

Ferdy Kaplan: "I think Herr Brod and I were subscribers to the same magazine. It seems that he too was following *Stylo Noir* and was reading articles about himself and Kafka."

Kommissar Müller: "Yes, that is a possibility."

Ferdy Kaplan: "I knew that *Stylo Noir* was much read in France, but I wasn't aware that its following had spread as far as Israel."

Kommissar Müller: "Herr Kaplan, from what you are saying, I would like to believe you are simply a reader of the magazine and do not have any direct link to it."

Ferdy Kaplan: "You should believe that."

Kommissar Müller: "When you were listening to Herr Brod's words, did any other possibility appear in your mind?"

Ferdy Kaplan: "Herr Brod must have been struck by that article in the magazine and have words such as God, Satan and willpower etched upon his mind. Just as I did. What else is possible?"

Kommissar Müller: "Since you thought that perhaps I had written Herr Brod's letter, well, I could have had the same thought about you."

Ferdy Kaplan: "You mean that I wrote that letter? How would it be possible for me to do that from here?"

Kommissar Müller: "I know that it would not have been possible. That is why I wiped it from my mind and was left with only one possibility."

Ferdy Kaplan: "What is that possibility?"

Kommissar Müller: "It is about the true identity of the person who wrote the text . . ."

Ferdy Kaplan: "You mean the article in the magazine?"

Kommissar Müller: "Yes."

Ferdy Kaplan: "Who wrote it? And more to the point, what significance does it have here?"

Kommissar Müller: "It was of no significance before, but now it has become very significant."

Ferdy Kaplan: "Why?"

Kommissar Müller: "Let me ask you a question, so you can contemplate it and weigh it up, as I have been doing all night long."

Ferdy Kaplan: "I admit to being curious about your question."

Kommissar Müller: "Herr Kaplan, do you think that Max Brod himself may have written that article in the magazine? What do you say?"

Ferdy Kaplan: "Herr Müller, are you trying to test me?"

Kommissar Müller: "Don't dismiss the idea straight away, think about it for a while and let its validity settle."

Ferdy Kaplan: "I can't read your expression because of the tiredness on your face. Are you serious about this?"

Kommissar Müller: "In my opinion, Herr Brod's letter harbours a lot more signs than we first thought."

Ferdy Kaplan: "You *are* serious."

Kommissar Müller: "The articles in *Stylo Noir* were written under pseudonyms, so why shouldn't Max Brod be the author of one of them?"

Ferdy Kaplan: "So, your point is that Herr Brod wrote articles to discredit himself. That doesn't seem to me to be a very persuasive argument."

Kommissar Müller: "Didn't Herr Brod do the same thing yesterday? In the letter he used critical words about himself and expressed his remorse."

Ferdy Kaplan: "I found his letter to be very sincere."

Kommissar Müller: "It is sincere, yes, that's why it reveals the truth."

Ferdy Kaplan: "But the article in the magazine did not stop at criticism; it also mentioned paying the price. In your opinion, Herr Brod wrote to the magazine to promote the idea that he should be punished for his actions. Is my understanding correct?"

Kommissar Müller: "Yes."

Ferdy Kaplan: "How strange."

[*Ferdy Kaplan closes his eyes and lowers his head. He places his hand on his right temple.*]

Kommissar Müller: "What is wrong? Are you confused or upset?"

Ferdy Kaplan: "I have a headache, that's all."

Kommissar Müller: "Is that really all?"

Ferdy Kaplan: "Yes, it's a headache."

After several sleepless nights in front of the postcard of Istanbul, Amalya sat down at her desk. In a long letter to Ferdy she wrote, "I don't know how to write briefly." She invited him to Paris and attached a poem to the end of her letter. "*You are Fate / You came from far away / Riding the horse of time / So far away once again / Come, that I may know / You are Fate.*" While she was waiting for Ferdy, Amalya cut her hair. She rearranged her room. She bought a drawing table for Ferdy and placed paints, brushes and pens upon it. She went to the airport and upon seeing Ferdy she gave him a big hug and held him in her arms for a very long time. Then she asked him the question that she had not asked in Istanbul: "Are you still having headaches?" Ferdy replied with surprise in his voice, "Not so often as before. Now and again." Amalya touched Ferdy's right temple, then kissed him on the lips. Together they joined the young people of Paris. They roamed the night bars filled with cigarette smoke and lively conversation, and this time they read Kafka's books in French.

Ferdy drew a portrait of Kafka with a black pen and

hung it on the wall. On the picture, he wrote "*Franz K.*" When Dr Hugo came to their room the next day, he asked Ferdy why he had written Kafka's name in that way. "In the Will that he left," Ferdy explained, "he made it clear that he didn't want to be known as 'the author Kafka' anymore. You know, in some novels he used only the initial *K* as the name of the protagonist. It was the *K* for Kafka and it was a mirror of his own self that he never revealed. During our years in Istanbul, Amalya and I called him Franz and loved him by that name. Now we feel that has a significance. Calling him by his first name is respecting his right to be known for himself. For us, he is not the author Kafka, but any other world citizen called Franz. He is Franz K."

Picking up a pen, Dr Hugo approached the picture and added the words "Lovers of". The caption on the picture now read "*Lovers of Franz K.*" Ferdy looked at Amalya with a smile. Then he asked Dr Hugo about the debate brewing in *Stylo Noir* magazine and wanted to know his thoughts on Max Brod. "I believe in the arguments developed by the philosopher Immanuel Kant," Dr Hugo said. "In one of his articles, Kant explains that even a person being chased by a lunatic murderer and whose life is in danger must not tell a lie. Lies protect no-one long-term; the truth will always come out." Dr Hugo went on to tell them about the life of the poet Louis Aragon. Aragon was born in Paris and lived with his mother and grandmother, although he knew them as his elder sister and his foster mother. His father, who visited them occasionally, was his godfather, he thought. His father was married to someone else, so he refused to marry Aragon's mother and be a father to him. When Aragon was nineteen and about to join the army and go off to the First World War, they told him the truth. Your sister is your mother, they said, your foster mother is your grandmother, and your godfather is actually your father. It was a time when those who set off to war were not expected to return, and so, as they prepared to send him into the arms of death, they revealed the truth to him. For Kant, truth sat above everything else: above fear, above love, above death, even. The Aragon family acted accordingly, as the breath of death came closer to them. "In my opinion," Dr Hugo went on, "Max Brod did not remain loyal to the truth. He took no notice of human nature and ignored the wishes of his friend. It is a responsibility of life to stay faithful to the truth. Kafka looked at the world in the same way that he looked at his authoritative father, and felt helpless. He wrote letters to this world he could not cope with, letters that he would never send. Max Brod did not understand Kafka. We discussed this matter in *Axiome*, the magazine we published during the war. Aragon, who survived the First World War, joined the Resistance during the Second World War and contributed to our magazine. That is when he told me his life story. We did not know each other's real names at that time, as everyone in the Resistance had an alias."

Kommissar Müller: "When I told Herr Brod he was obliged to attend court, I should have been suspicious of his immediate acquiescence. He distracted us so that he could leave Berlin without attracting attention."

Ferdy Kaplan: "It seems he did not want to be subjected to the prosecutor's questions and embroiled in a new debate about Kafka."

Kommissar Müller: "I am no longer taking into consideration the presumptions of the prosecutor. Neither the idea of a link between *Axiome* and *Stylo Noir*, nor the interference of East Germany . . ."

Ferdy Kaplan: "So you are altogether confident in your new argument?"

Kommissar Müller: "I think that Herr Brod did not want to be confronted by you. The exchange that would have taken place between the two of you might have led to the disclosure of his game."

Ferdy Kaplan: "Kommissar Müller, isn't this a very sudden change of direction on your part? How did such a short letter come to change your thinking?"

Kommissar Müller: "Why are you surprised by this? It was you who spoke yesterday about drawing long conclusions from short letters."

Ferdy Kaplan: "That is not the same thing."

Kommissar Müller: "If only I had changed my mind earlier, I might have prevented Herr Brod from running away."

Ferdy Kaplan: "How could you have changed your mind? You focused on the wrong things from the very beginning."

Kommissar Müller: "Having seen a young victim on the scene and caught an assailant red-handed, I saw everything too simply. Just as I ignored what you said, I also ignored some of the reports that reached us."

Ferdy Kaplan: "What reports?"

Kommissar Müller: "Yesterday, when I was listening to Herr Brod's letter, I became aware of an earlier mistake of mine. I remembered a note from the French police. They said that it was important, but for some reason I did not find it relevant to our case."

Ferdy Kaplan: "What was it about?"

Kommissar Müller: "They said that letters from Tel Aviv would often be delivered to *Stylo Noir* magazine."

Ferdy Kaplan: "From Tel Aviv?"

Kommissar Müller: "That surprises you, does it not?"

Ferdy Kaplan: "I cannot deny that I am surprised."

Kommissar Müller: "The French police said that the letters contained readers' comments and articles for publication."

Ferdy Kaplan: "Please go on."

Kommissar Müller: "I think that you and I are about to reach a consensus for the first time. Before we go any further, have a cigarette."

[*Kommissar Müller offers Ferdy Kaplan a cigarette.*]

Ferdy Kaplan: "I'm all ears."

Kommissar Müller: "The articles defending Kafka and criticising Max Brod mostly came in these letters. And it was Herr Brod himself who wrote them, under a pseudonym. Logic leads me to this conclusion."

Ferdy Kaplan: "I can understand Herr Brod suffering a crisis of conscience, but still, isn't it an extreme scenario that he should plot his own murder?"

Kommissar Müller: "At the time of his death, Kafka was unknown, but Brod was famous. Now the situation is reversed. While everyone knows Kafka, Brod's name has been forgotten. Herr Brod seems to have desired an honourable death, to ensure that his name would shine once more."

Ferdy Kaplan: "And I was to be the one to grant him that glory."

Kommissar Müller: "As I was listening to his letter being read in the courtroom, I remembered the note from the French police. Then I saw that it was not you but Herr Brod himself who wrote the article in the magazine."

Ferdy Kaplan: "And at the end of his letter to the court he emphasised that he wished he had died in the place of that young man."

Kommissar Müller: "That was his true wish, Herr Kaplan."

Ferdy Kaplan: "Now I understand."

Kommissar Müller: "It is also clear that Herr Brod agreed with you. He believed that he should be punished, which means he adopted your truth."

Ferdy Kaplan: "By your argument, the very opposite is the case. It was not my truth, but that of Herr Brod, as he had spread the idea through his articles in the magazine."

Kommissar Müller: "At the time of the surveys, in particular, readers' letters from Israel poured in. The French police initially saw that as an indication of his popularity in Israel, as a Jewish writer."

Ferdy Kaplan: "It is possible. Readers from Israel took a special interest in Kafka, and were not so fond of Herr Brod, perhaps. It may be that reports of the survey appeared in the Israeli press, and people heard about it."

Kommissar Müller: "This is just an supposition; there is no evidence for that."

Ferdy Kaplan: "Yours is also an supposition. If Herr Brod had been behind all this, the French police would have worked it out, would they not? In the reports they shared with you, did they state Herr Brod's direct involvement in these events?"

Kommissar Müller: "No, his name is not mentioned in their reports."

Ferdy Kaplan: "You yourself are interpreting what they did not say."

Kommissar Müller: "I understand that you find it difficult to believe. In the beginning, I too could not bring myself to accept the obvious facts. Now I have come to a totally different conclusion."

Ferdy Kaplan: "And does the prosecutor think the same? Does he share your hypothesis?"

Kommissar Müller: "He has not heard it yet. This is something only we know, those of us here: you, me and my colleagues. I have spent the whole night trying to convince them."

[*Kommissar Müller looks at his fellow officers.*]

Ferdy Kaplan: "It seems that your officers are finding it hard to believe you, just as I am. Look at their faces . . ."

Kommissar Müller: "They are tired, they need to rest. That's all."

Ferdy Kaplan: "We are all tired."

Kommissar Müller: "Yes, Herr Kaplan. [*Kommissar Müller looks at his watch.*] Now go and rest for a couple of hours. We will return to take you to the hearing."

Ferdy Kaplan: "I need to gather my thoughts with a clear head. That way I'll be able to see better where you have gone wrong."

Kommissar Müller: "I think today is not my day for being mistaken."

Ferdy Kaplan: "I will see you later."

Kommissar Müller: "Lie down and close your eyes. Even if you can't sleep, it will be good for your headache."

7

WEST BERLIN
FROM THE PRISON TO
THE COURTHOUSE

As the city of Berlin burns once again under the midday sun, three prison vehicles take Ferdy Kaplan to the courthouse. Due to the intense heat, everyone is either in their place of work or at home; the streets are deserted. A heavy smell of mould and damp emanates from the wall that splits the city.

Kommissar Müller sits next to Ferdy Kaplan in the middle vehicle of the convoy.

Kommissar Müller: "Did you manage to sleep?"

Ferdy Kaplan: "For two hours? How is that possible?"

Kommissar Müller: "And your headache?"

Ferdy Kaplan: "It's a little less painful now."

Kommissar Müller: "A rest has been helpful, then."

Ferdy Kaplan: "Kommissar Müller, you are starting to be kind to me."

Kommissar Müller: "The closer one gets to the truth, the gentler one becomes. There are some secrets you have not revealed to us, and yet we have what we need for now. Your case is not like any other murder inquiry. Although I consider what you did to be wrong, I am trying to understand you."

Ferdy Kaplan: "Good cop . . ."

Kommissar Müller: "No, that's not right. I am not playing the good cop, bad cop trick."

Ferdy Kaplan: "Today I believe what you say. What about you, did you get some rest?"

Kommissar Müller: "You see, you are being kinder to me, too."

Ferdy Kaplan: "Day by day, I am becoming more like you."

Kommissar Müller: "I didn't have time to rest. I was on the telephone with the Paris police."

Ferdy Kaplan: "Did you get anything useful from them?"

Kommissar Müller: "I told them I didn't have time to wait days on end for new reports and I explained the conclusions I had drawn. They confirmed that some of the articles for *Stylo Noir* were posted from Tel Aviv. And, during the days of the 'Should Max Brod pay the price?' survey, responses flooded in from Tel Aviv and other cities in Israel. They, too, think that these letters determined the outcome of the survey. I told them of my opinion that it was Max Brod himself who was behind all this. Although they would not at this point be able to include that in their report, they told me they shared my opinion."

Ferdy Kaplan: "In effect, they said you were right?"

Kommissar Müller: "Yes, they said that clearly. Herr Kaplan, I am hoping that you too will accept that I am right."

Ferdy Kaplan: "I accept what you said."

Kommissar Müller: "Really?"

Ferdy Kaplan: "Yes, really."

Kommissar Müller: "So I have succeeded in convincing you. At last. For the first time I am one step ahead of you in this case."

Ferdy Kaplan: "We can say that, yes, you are ahead of me. But it is not your arguments that convinced me to accept that theory."

Kommissar Müller: "What does that mean?"

Ferdy Kaplan: "I myself found a piece of evidence. That is what eventually convinced me."

Kommissar Müller: "If you didn't believe me, what changed your mind?"

Ferdy Kaplan: "No, that's not what I meant to say. I believed you, but I kept looking for a weak point in your words, a flaw in your argument, until I realised something. It is so strange that I did not work it out before . . ."

Kommissar Müller: "What did you realise?"

Ferdy Kaplan: "Dante."

Kommissar Müller: "Dante?"

Ferdy Kaplan: "It's something I hadn't paid attention to before. This morning, when I was being escorted back to my cell after talking to you, I walked through a dimly lit corridor, a on guard either side of me. The ceiling of the corridor was low; it felt as though I was entering a tomb. The walls were filthy, the plaster was flaking and the smell of urine was everywhere. From behind the iron doors came moans. The sound of the guards' boots echoed on the concrete, and it felt to me like the sound of the demons' hooves in hell. At that moment I remembered the Inferno, the hell of Dante's book. Herr Brod mentioned it in his letter."

Kommissar Müller: "So what of it? You too have mentioned Dante. The source was the article in *Stylo Noir*. It was used there."

Ferdy Kaplan: "This morning, when you said that Herr Brod might have been the author of that article in the magazine, my mind went blank for a while. But later I remembered that sentence in Herr Brod's letter."

Kommissar Müller: "An ordinary sentence . . ."

Ferdy Kaplan: "Yes, Herr Brod said something ordinary and referred to Dante's book as the *Comedy*."

Kommissar Müller: "I wonder what conclusion you are going to draw from this."

Ferdy Kaplan: "The title of Dante's book is *The Divine Comedy*. It has been published for centuries under this name. That is how it is known."

Kommissar Müller: "They taught us that in high school."

Ferdy Kaplan: "They taught you wrong."

Kommissar Müller: "What's wrong with that?"

Ferdy Kaplan: "Dante didn't name his book *The Divine Comedy*, he called it simply *The Comedy*. He too had a Brod figure who appeared after his death. The Italian writer Boccaccio, while giving lectures and writing papers on Dante's *Comedy*, added the word 'divine' to the title of the book. He turned *The Comedy* into *The Divine Comedy*."

Kommissar Müller: "They didn't teach us that at school."

Ferdy Kaplan: "Dante died a year after he finished *The Comedy*. Boccaccio was a young child at the time. He grew up, became a famous writer and went against the wishes of a dead writer by changing the name of his work."

Kommissar Müller: "The world of literature seems to be filled with strange crimes . . ."

Ferdy Kaplan: "Crime! You have used the right word and now, for the first time, you begin to think like me."

Kommissar Müller: "When I said 'crime', I didn't mean go and kill someone."

Ferdy Kaplan: "Boccaccio has been dead for centuries. No need to worry about him."

Kommissar Müller: "I used to feel it was a pity I couldn't find the time to read literature, but now I feel almost grateful that I stayed away from that world."

Ferdy Kaplan: "We should prevent the murder of a writer's soul when their physical body is no longer with us. Bear this in mind, will you, Herr Müller?"

Kommissar Müller: "If everyone does whatever they want . . . I don't understand, no, such a thing doesn't make sense . . . Imagine a literary figure changing Goethe's *Faust* 100 years later, or 200 years . . ."

Ferdy Kaplan: "*Divine Faust* . . ."

Kommissar Müller: "I can't believe that."

Ferdy Kaplan: "It's those Brod figures you believe in, they bring these things into existence."

Kommissar Müller: "Do you think, then, that Herr Brod knows what happened to Dante's book?"

Ferdy Kaplan: "Yes, he knew that Dante, like Kafka, was a victim of injustice, and, in this way, he compared himself to Boccaccio. Because he felt guilty, he wrote an article in which he mentioned Dante and sent it to *Stylo Noir*. He did the same thing in the letter he sent to the court, by not referring to Dante's book by its changed name. He didn't use the word 'divine', I mean. He was loyal to the author and called it *Comedy*. In this way he showed his fidelity to the truth. I realised this as I was walking back to my cell in the dimly lit corridor, and that's when I believed you were right."

Kommissar Müller: "If that is so, not even dying can save writers; anything can happen to them at any time."

Ferdy Kaplan: "Dead writers have nobody but us, the readers. Justice and mercy are in our hands, not in the hands of the courts."

Kommissar Müller: "You see, Herr Brod did not believe in the courts either. He believed in the readers, and he wanted the readers themselves to punish him."

Ferdy Kaplan: "Herr Müller, do you know who I'm thinking of right now?"

Kommissar Müller: "Who?"

Ferdy Kaplan: "Young Ernest Fischer. I feel so sorry for his parents . . ."

Kommissar Müller: "After what you have learnt, would you still hunt down Max Brod?"

Ferdy Kaplan: "If I had the opportunity, I would go after him because of Ernest Fischer, not because of Kafka."

Kommissar Müller: "What happened to the tradition?"

Ferdy Kaplan: "What tradition?"

Kommissar Müller: "The tradition that gives a man freedom to live if their rope at the gallows breaks . . ."

Ferdy Kaplan: "You are right, Kommissar Müller, today you are quite right. Let me ask you something. Do you think that Herr Brod had anything to do with the debate on Kafka that began all those years ago in *Axiome* magazine?"

Kommissar Müller: "He had no connection with that magazine. But he heard about the debate and became aware of the survey, 'Should Kafka be burned?' As he grew older, he began to question what he had done, and then he remembered that debate. Using *Axiome* as his model, he sent that letter to *Stylo Noir.*"

Ferdy Kaplan: "Is this your opinion? Or is that what the reports from France are saying?"

Kommissar Müller: "It's not in the reports, but I asked the French police about it this morning. They said that the first debate about Kafka was the idea of the members of the Resistance who published *Axiome.*"

Ferdy Kaplan: "I'm glad to hear that."

Kommissar Müller: "Are you glad to hear that? What does it matter now?"

Ferdy Kaplan: "Think of Herr Brod: he shaped Kafka's fate, influenced *Stylo Noir* magazine, and, as if that was not enough, he mapped out his own death. But your words mean that there was at least one place the man's hand could not reach, and I am glad to hear that. Do you know that when Kafka was still a young man, before he had published anything, Brod named Kafka among the greatest writers of his time in his article for *Die Gegenwart* magazine, published here in Berlin. Even at that early stage, Brod decided to etch the name of an unknown civil servant from Prague into the history books. Anything can be expected from a person of such fervour."

Kommissar Müller: "I would not be surprised to find he had some involvement with *Axiome* magazine as well."

Ferdy Kaplan: "Herr Müller, when I emerged alive from the rubble during the war, I believed that anything was possible in life. I believe that now more than ever."

Kommissar Müller: "I have cultivated the same belief in my profession."

Ferdy Kaplan: "I want to ask you something: do your vehicles always follow the same route? Is there no other way? If only you had gone through my neighbourhood, around Steglitz or Grunewald. I so wanted to see those places."

Kommissar Müller: "What are you saying? Remember, this is a prison vehicle, not a tourist bus. Besides, you live in Steglitz. What business have you got in Grunewald?"

Ferdy Kaplan: "Kafka and my grandfather both lived in that district."

Kommissar Müller: "Did Kafka live in Berlin? This is something new. I think I should stop researching Max Brod's life and concentrate a little more on Kafka's."

Ferdy Kaplan: "I too found out much later that Kafka lived here. I don't know if my grandfather was actually acquainted with him, but the story he told me about Kafka, when he was seeing me off to Istanbul, was not a story that would have been known by just anyone at the time."

Kommissar Müller: "What story is that?"

Ferdy Kaplan: "Kafka spent the final year of his life in Berlin with his lover, Dora. They lived in the Steglitz neighbourhood. They had financial difficulties and were also contending with an awful landlord. Afterwards, they moved to Grunewald Street."

Kommissar Müller: "And the story your grandfather told you . . . ?"

Ferdy Kaplan: "You are becoming more interested in stories, Herr Müller."

Kommissar Müller: "How could I not, after all this?"

Ferdy Kaplan: "One day, as Kafka and Dora were walking in the park, they came across a little girl who was crying because she had lost her doll. Kafka tried to comfort the girl, telling her that her doll had not been lost, but that it was bored living with the same family and had decided to go on a journey. 'I know this because your doll sent me a letter,' he said. The little girl looked at him in disbelief and asked him to prove it. The next day, Kafka arrived with a letter in his hand. The letters went on for three weeks, and in the final one the doll wrote that it had met a man and had married him."

Kommissar Müller: "It seems that Kafka was fond of children."

Ferdy Kaplan: "So was my grandfather. When he told me this story about Kafka, he elaborated on it in his own way. In his version, Kafka came back with a doll and told the little girl that her doll had returned. By adding this ending to the story, my grandfather was trying to give me hope. But Kafka did not try to give hope to anyone. On the contrary, he showed the suffocating side of life. I discovered the original story when I read memoirs about Dora. It happened 40 years ago, right here in this city. My grandfather was living around here too, at that time."

Kommissar Müller: "Dora . . . do you think I should read up on her too?"

Ferdy Kaplan: "If you want to see someone wholeheartedly devoted to Kafka, you must know Dora. When Kafka's tuberculosis was worsening, Dora found a place for him in a sanatorium near Vienna. As he took his last breath, Dora brought him a bunch of flowers. Kafka opened his eyes, smelled the flowers . . . and, well . . ."

Kommissar Müller: "That is how he died?"

[*The prison convoy slows down as it enters a quiet street and comes to a halt.*]

Ferdy Kaplan: "Yes, that is how he died. Dora was the only person who believed that people should respect Kafka himself, not his works. For that reason, she spoke out against the publication of his books. She said as much to Max Brod, too."

Kommissar Müller: "Herr Kaplan, we cannot change our route, but tomorrow I will go have a look around the places where Kafka, Dora and your grandfather once walked, and I will tell you what I have seen."

Ferdy Kaplan: "Thank you."

[*The prison convoy continues to wait, stationary.*]

Kommissar Müller: "What's up? What are we waiting for?"

[*Kommissar Müller leans forward from the back seat and sees a broken-down white minibus blocking the road ahead. The driver of the minibus is under the bonnet, busying himself with the engine. A guard from the lead prison van gets out to give him a hand. At that moment, armed men jump out of the minibus'*] *rear door. Several others pour out from a shop on the corner and join them. Some have shotguns, others have handguns. Their faces are covered by masks or scarves. They do not speak and communicate only with gestures. They apprehend the prison guard who has come to the help of the driver. They surround the convoy. Among them is a woman with short hair. The woman points her gun and walks confidently. She approaches the middle vehicle. When Kommissar Müller sees her coming, he draws his weapon.*]

Kommissar Müller: "For God's sake! What's that? Wait for my signal!"

[*The two officers in the front seats also draw their guns.*]

Ferdy Kaplan: "Don't try it. You stand no chance."

Kommissar Müller: "I can see that. But I'm not willing to be a sitting duck either."

Ferdy Kaplan: "Don't you see you are surrounded?"

Kommissar Müller: "You were expecting this, weren't you, you knew all about it . . ."

Ferdy Kaplan: "How could I know about it? You transferred me to a different prison. How could anyone communicate with me?"

Kommissar Müller: "I will find out how this happened."

Ferdy Kaplan: "I asked you if you could change the route; only a moment ago I suggested that you go through other neighbourhoods. Had I known about this, would I have said that to you?"

As he was getting used to Paris and his new life there, Ferdy's headaches began to worsen. He tried to manage with the medicines he had, but when they became ineffective, he went to the hospital to consult Dr Hugo. He told him that as a child during the war he had been wounded, and a piece of shrapnel had lodged in his head. Dr Hugo took an X-ray, examined him and consulted his colleagues.

"You have a tumour in your brain," he said. "That is why you are having such severe headaches. You need surgery, but I have to tell you, it is the kind of operation that carries risk."

Ferdy said that he did not want surgery and asked a favour of Dr Hugo. "Can we please not mention a word of this to Amalya and Eliz?"

Dr Hugo agreed. "We won't tell them, but if they suspect and ask, we'll have to tell them the truth."

Ferdy nodded. "You know, Doctor, Amalya told me about your family and your village. You seem not to forget the numbers. I don't forget the numbers either. We are alike in that, you and I. You were following the trail of the second informant who targeted your village, you and your friends. Are you still looking for him?"

Dr Hugo said, "Yes, we are still after him. The man is moving fast, he keeps switching his location, he always manages to slip away at the last minute."

Ferdy held his breath for a moment, then said, "I would like to join your team."

The doctor discouraged him. "What? In your condition? No, that is not possible."

Ferdy insisted. "My health has no importance, I want to do something with you. Actually, we both want to."

This further surprised Dr Hugo. "By both, do you mean you and Amalya?"

"Yes," Ferdy said.

Dr Hugo took Ferdy by the arm. "Let's talk about this later. Now, you should go and rest."

Ferdy walked the streets all day, alone. He hummed songs to himself. He sat on the bank of the Seine and watched the boats passing by, full of cheerful voices. When he woke up that night, he was drenched in sweat, and he told Amalya about the dream he had been having. "It's so strange," he said. "I had a similar dream many years ago. My mother was standing in an empty street, waiting motionless. I was a child. I ran to her. Don't leave me, Mama, I said. I was crying. My mother embraced me and told me to rest in her arms. I rested my head on her breast and that's when I woke up."

Amalya put out her hand in the dark room, touched his face and kissed him gently. She wrapped her arms around his neck and said, "We shall not spend a single day apart from each other, Ferdy."

They slept together, they awoke together. They laughed, they strolled. They went to the cinema, they read books.

While reading Kafka's last story, *A Hunger Artist*, they decided to write letters to the dead. Writing letters to the dead was a sign of the respect they had for life. Because the Hunger Artist said, "Forgive me!" before he died in Kafka's story, they wrote him a postcard with the words: "We forgive you, and you forgive us too!" They posted the card to the publisher of the story. They wrote a card to Kafka and sent it to the New Jewish Cemetery in Prague. Then it was time to write to people they had known. Ferdy wrote a card to his grandparents and sent it to the Merkez Efendi Cemetery in Istanbul. He posted a card to his Berliner grandfather at Steglitz Cemetery and a card to his parents with the address of the house where they had died. Amalya wrote a long letter to her father. A pilot, he had died when she was five. She sent it to the Mediterranean Sea, where his plane had crashed in the middle of the night. The address on the envelope was simple: "The Mediterranean Sea, Middle of the Night." The rest was in the hands of the postmen.

Kommissar Müller: "Herr Kaplan, I seem to have underestimated your intelligence."

Ferdy Kaplan: "I am telling the truth. I knew nothing about this."

Kommissar Müller: "Alright. Now, let's get on with our work."

Ferdy Kaplan: "You will gain nothing by fighting."

Kommissar Müller: "Who cares about gain?"

Ferdy Kaplan: "Please, Herr Müller, I don't want you to come to any harm."

Kommissar Müller: "You're thinking of me? There's no need, I am simply doing my job."

Ferdy Kaplan: "I am thinking of your safety, thinking of you and your wife. Listen, an innocent student died. If you put up a fight, the same might happen to you. Your colleagues here will die too."

Kommissar Müller: "You are not thinking of yourself, then?"

Ferdy Kaplan: "I have long since stopped thinking about myself. Just take a look outside . . ."

[*Kommissar Müller wipes the sweat from his brow and looks at the two officers sitting in front of him.*]

Kommissar Müller: "I see that we have no chance."

Ferdy Kaplan: "Don't let anyone get hurt. They have already caught one of your colleagues."

Kommissar Müller: "I don't want any of my men to come to harm."

Ferdy Kaplan: "If you let me go, everyone will be safe."

Kommissar Müller: "What about Max Brod?"

Ferdy Kaplan: "He will be safe too."

Kommissar Müller: "How am I supposed to believe you?"

Ferdy Kaplan: "I believe you, Herr Müller, and I know that deep in your heart you believe me, too."

Kommissar Müller: "Are you talking about a police officer and a killer believing in each other?"

Ferdy Kaplan: "I am talking about two people who understand each other, so believe in each other."

Kommissar Müller: "Ah, how have I fallen into this situation . . . ?"

Ferdy Kaplan: "Take one step back, just for once . . ."

Kommissar Müller: "For you?"

Ferdy Kaplan: "No, I'll say it again, for your colleagues and for your wife."

Kommissar Müller: "Not for myself . . ."

Ferdy Kaplan: "I know that you are willing to sacrifice yourself, but think of the others."

Kommissar Müller: "I am thinking of the others."

Ferdy Kaplan: "Yes, that's the right thing to do. This time, if you admit that I'm right . . ."

Kommissar Müller: "I see . . ."

Ferdy Kaplan: "Will you agree and say yes?"

Kommissar Müller: "Yes, Herr Kaplan."

Ferdy Kaplan: "That's the right thing to do."

Kommissar Müller: "Unfortunately, that does seem to be the case."

Ferdy Kaplan: "If your men in the front put down their guns . . ."

Kommissar Müller: "O.K., guys, put down your guns. There is no point in a fight."

Ferdy Kaplan: "I'm glad for you, really I am."

Kommissar Müller: "Herr Kaplan, I sense that it's not our lives you are thinking of but the life of that woman."

[*The woman with short hair comes over and holds her gun to the window.*]

Ferdy Kaplan: "Life is strange, Herr Müller, it's really strange . . ."

Kommissar Müller: "And you are a part of that strangeness, Herr Kaplan."

Ferdy Kaplan: "We all are."

[*The woman pulls the door open, sharply. "Come on, Ferdy!" she says in French. "Come on, we're going!"*]

Kommissar Müller: "Yes, she is exactly like her. If she takes her scarf off her face, it is as if Jean Seberg will appear."

Ferdy Kaplan: "This is the end of our journey, Herr Müller . . ."

Kommissar Müller: "I still don't understand, Herr Kaplan. On the one hand you are interested in art and literature, and on the other, in this violence . . ."

Ferdy Kaplan: "You know, during the Nazi era too, people were rescued in this way from courtrooms and prisons."

Kommissar Müller: "The Nazis are long gone, yet you carry on with your old habits. You don't see that the world is changing."

Ferdy Kaplan: "You say the world is changing; if only you could change with it. For instance, if only you could become a bit more like your wife, if only you could become a little more French . . ."

[*The woman pokes her head into the vehicle. "Come on, Ferdy," she says, "We have no time."*]

Kommissar Müller: "I see that you have already become a little more French."

Ferdy Kaplan: "I have to go, Herr Müller. I hope that from now on you will take care of dead writers."

Kommissar Müller: "Only people like you can take care of those writers, Herr Kaplan. My wife is a good reader, she will help to take care of them. There is no need for guns."

[*The woman leans into the van curiously. She looks Kommissar Müller in the eyes. Then she touches Ferdy Kaplan on his right temple and asks, "Are you alright?" Without waiting for an answer, she grabs Ferdy's handcuffed hands and pulls him out of the car.*]

Ferdy Kaplan: "Farewell, Herr Müller."

Kommissar Müller: "Perhaps we will meet again, Herr Kaplan."

Ferdy Kaplan: "Who can say?"

8

TOWARDS THE END

With Ferdy Kaplan on board, the white minibus dives into the streets and disappears from sight into this city of long and silent walls.

Two months later, a postcard with Ernest Fischer's name on it arrives at the cemetery where he was laid to rest. On the front of the card is a hand-drawn sketch of a fishing boat, a flock of seagulls and a cracked sun. On the back are some lines by the poet Aragon, descending like the rungs of a ladder:

> *I am going to tell you a great secret*
> *Time is you*
>
> *. . .*
>
> *Time*
> *like an endless mane of hair*
> *Combed*
> *A mirror that breath mists and demists*

Time is you
who sleeps at dawn while I awaken
It is you like a knife across my throat
. . .

I am going to tell you a great secret
Shut the doors
It is easier to die than to love
That's why I give myself to the misery of living
My love

The same day, an envelope addressed to Kommissar Müller arrives at the police station on Friesenstrasse, with a book inside: *The Divine Comedy*. The word "Divine" is crossed out with red pen. An inscription is written with the same pen on the first page:

"To Frau Müller and Herr Müller, for the beauty of the art and kindness of people . . ."

A few months later, on December 20, Max Brod closes his eyes for the final time and dies in Tel Aviv. In his Will, he leaves his entire archive, including Kafka's works, to his secretary, asking her to donate them to a public institution. His secretary disregards his Will and transfers all the works to her private ownership, and when she dies, she bequeaths them to her daughters. For the next 50 years, there will be disputes and legal cases over Max Brod's Will.

Shortly after Max Brod's death, a postcard arrives at his grave in Trumpeldor Cemetery. On the front of the card is a hand-drawn portrait of Kafka and on the back, just four words:

"I love you, Max."